This igloo book belongs to:

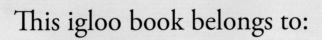

....

igloobooks
.com

Published in 2012
by Igloo Books Ltd
Cottage Farm
Sywell
NN6 0BJ
www.igloobooks.com

SHE001 0912
10 9 8 7 6 5 4 3 2 1
ISBN 978-0-85780-762-5

Project managed by Brierley Books

Illustrated by: Simone Abel, Jackie East, Masumi Furukawa, Paige Billin-Frye,
Paula Knight, Kim Martin, Barbara Vagnozzi, Liza Woodruff
Cover by Kim Martin

Original stories and re-tellings by: Laurence Burden, Gaby Goldsack, Patrice Lawrence,
Sue McMillan, Alison Morris, Louise Rooney, Linda Watters

Printed and manufactured in China

Stories
for
Girls

igloobooks
.com

Contents

Stories for Younger Girls

Thumbelina . . . . pages 6-13

Trouble . . . . . . pages 14-19

Wilfred Wolfred . . . . pages 20-27

The Golden Goose . . . . pages 28-37

The Adventures of Tiny Pony . . . . pages 38-45

The Elves & the Shoemaker . . . . . . pages 46-53

The Magic Dancing Shoes . . . . pages 54-63

Little Red Hen . . . . . . pages 64-67

Snowfall the Unicorn . . . . pages 68-73

Chicken Little . . . . . . pages 74-77

Stories for Older Girls

Treasure Island . . . . pages 78-85

Snow White & Rose Red . . . . pages 86-93

The Missing Pony . . . . pages 94-101

Clever Manka . . . . pages 102-111

The Robot Nan . . . . page 112-119

The Six Swans . . . . page 120-127

The Bee Wing Ball Gown . . . . page 128-135

The Fisherman & His Wife . . . . page 136-143

The Butterfly Garden . . . . page 144-151

The Little Mermaid . . . . page 152-160

Thumbelina

Once there was a wife who longed for a little girl. So she went to see an old wise woman, to ask for her help. "I wish for a little girl more than anything in the world," sighed the wife. "Won't you please help me?"

"With all my heart," replied the kindly old woman, and she gave the wife a barley seed. "This is not like the seed the farmer sows," said the old woman. "This is a special seed, which you must take home and plant in a pot."

The wife took the seed and planted it. Soon a beautiful yellow and red flower grew. The wife thought it so beautiful that she couldn't help kissing it. At once, the petals unfurled. There in the middle sat a delicate girl with golden hair. She was tiny, smaller even than a thumb, so the wife named her Thumbelina.

The wife and tiny girl were happy together. During the day, Thumbelina played on the table, singing songs in her sweet voice. At night, she slept soundly in a bed made from a walnut shell, with rose-petal blankets.

One night an ugly toad came hopping in through the window and saw Thumbelina asleep. "What a pretty wife she will make for my son," she said, and she picked up the bed, then hopped out of the window, down to the stream. She placed the bed on a water lily. "She cannot escape from here," thought the toad.

When Thumbelina awoke and saw where she was she began to cry.
"Dry your tears," croaked the toad, swimming over. "You are to marry my son, and you shall live together down in the mud."

But the toad's son was very ugly. Poor Thumbelina did not want to marry him. "Who will save me now?" she sobbed.

Luckily, the fish in the stream felt sorry for the beautiful girl. When the toad was sleeping, they chewed the stem of the lily leaf on which Thumbelina sat. At once, the flowing water carried Thumbelina and the leaf off down stream, far way from the ugly toads.

She was just beginning to feel happy again, when suddenly a large beetle buzzed down, seized her and flew high into a tree. Finally, he put her down on a leaf. "How pretty you are," the beetle told the tiny girl. "Would you like some honey?" It wasn't long before the other lady beetles heard about the tiny girl, and came to see Thumbelina for themselves.
"She only has two legs. How ugly!" laughed one, giving Thumbelina a prod. "Look! She has no feelers," cried another. "How odd!" Embarrassed by their laughter, the male beetle picked up the tiny girl and set her down on a daisy in the field below.

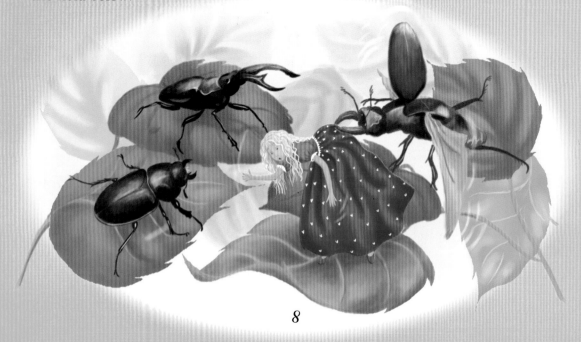

All summer and autumn Thumbelina lived in the wood. She made a bed from grass, sheltered by a leaf. She ate nectar from the flowers, drank dew from the leaves and sang with the birds.

When winter arrived it grew very cold. The birds flew away, leaving Thumbelina alone. Her clothes were worn and she could find nothing to wrap around herself. She was also very hungry; she had to find food and shelter for the winter. She walked through the wood until she came to a hole where a field mouse lived. Thumbelina knocked on the door.

When the kindly mouse saw the little girl, she was filled with pity. "Come in, child," she said. "You must be frozen."

The mouse listened in silence as Thumbelina told her story. Then she smiled. "Why don't you come and live with me?" she suggested. "To repay me, you can help to clean my house, tell me stories and sing me songs."

So Thumbelina stayed with the mouse and did what she was asked. One day the mouse told Thumbelina that her friend the mole would be visiting. "He is most handsome," she said. "He would make you a fine husband."

When the mole arrived, he took quite a fancy to Thumbelina.
"This is a passage between my home and yours," he said, showing Thumbelina a dark tunnel. "You are most welcome to use it to visit me anytime. But do be careful. There is a dead bird in there."

Thumbelina looked into the tunnel. There on the floor lay a dead swallow. When she saw the poor bird, tears filled her eyes. "I will bring him a cover," she whispered, stroking its feathers.

As Thumbelina placed the cover over the swallow, she was surprised to feel his heart beating. The tiny girl was filled with joy. The bird was alive!

All through the long winter, Thumbelina cared for the swallow. Finally, when spring arrived, Thumbelina knew her friend was strong enough to fly once more. "It's time for you to leave," said Thumbelina bravely. Then she made a hole in the roof of the tunnel, so the swallow could escape.

"Why don't you come with me," said the swallow. But Thumbelina could not leave the mouse after all her kindness. So she gave the bird one last hug, then watched as her friend flew away.

That night, the mole asked Thumbelina to marry him. Although she did not want to, Thumbelina agreed, just to make the mouse happy.

Every evening the mole visited to talk about the wedding, as Thumbelina stitched her wedding clothes.
"My home is very snug," he would tell her. "No nasty bright sunlight at all." Thumbelina's heart sank. The more she listened, the unhappier she felt. How could she possibly live without the sun?

Finally, the day came when the mole came to fetch his wife and take her deep into his dark hole.

Thumbelina thought her heart might break.
"Goodbye sun," she cried, taking one last look at the sky. "Goodbye flowers." And she kissed a nearby daisy.

Suddenly, there was a fluttering of wings. Thumbelina looked up to see her
friend the swallow flying above.

"Oh, Swallow," she cried, "today I must say goodbye to the sunshine forever." And she told him all about the mole and his dark, dark home.

"Come with me," said the swallow. "It will be cold here again soon, but I am flying far away to a warm country, where the sun always shines."

"Yes, yes!" cried Thumbelina, climbing onto the swallow's back. "I could never
make the mole happy. He should marry Mouse instead."

The swallow soared into the air, swooping over mountains and forests, until at
last they came to a warm country, where the sun shone brightly. He came to rest
near a lake, where a ruined palace covered in trailing vines rose up into the sky.
"This is my home," said the swallow, placing Thumbelina
gently on the petals of a flower.

Thumbelina rubbed her eyes in amazement. There inside the flower sat a tiny young man no bigger than a thumb, with gossamer wings. As soon as she laid eyes on him, Thumbelina fell instantly in love.

"I am the King of the flower spirits," said the tiny man, gazing at the beautiful girl before him. Then he took off his crown and placed it gently upon Thumbelina's head. "Will you be my bride and become Queen of the flower spirits?" he asked.

"With all my heart," replied Thumbelina, unable to believe how happy she felt.

At last, she had found her true home.

Trouble

On the morning of her seventh birthday, Katie awoke to find the cutest little kitten she had ever seen, sitting at the foot of her bed. The kitten was watching her with a curious look in his eyes.

"Hello!" said Katie. "What's your name?"

But the kitten just looked at her mischievously.

"Happy Birthday!" said Katie's mother, from the doorway. "He doesn't have a name yet. We thought you would like to decide."

"Thanks!" said Katie, leaping out of bed and giving her mother a huge hug. "He's just what I've been wishing for!"

Katie and the kitten bonded instantly. Though Katie received lots of other lovely gifts for her birthday, nothing compared to the little bundle of fur that bounced around the room.

"You need a name," said Katie, kissing the little kitten on his nose. But, try as she might, she couldn't decide what to call him. With her parents' help, she made a list of ideas – Cookie, Ginger, Fluffy – but none of the names were quite right.

When it was time to get ready for bed, Katie sat and brushed her hair, while the kitten lay on her bed and licked his paws.

"Have you thought of a name for your kitten yet?" asked Katie's mother, coming in. Katie shook her head.

15

Trouble

"Why don't you think overnight?" suggested Katie's mother. "I'm sure you'll have thought of one by tomorrow. Now, it's time for him to come downstairs so you can go to bed."

"But he wants to sleep in here with me!" Katie protested. "He told me so!"

"The decision is final," Katie's mother replied. "He'll sleep fine downstairs in the hall in his snug new basket," she promised.

But nobody got a wink of sleep that night, especially not the kitten. All night long he mewed and mewed and mewed. In the morning, Katie's parents decided that they would have to move the kitten into the living room.

"Perhaps it was too cold for him in the hall," said her mother. "At least if he is in the living room, the noise will be muffled, so he won't keep everyone awake."

Katie cuddled the kitten and stroked his fur.

"I'm sorry," she whispered in his ear. "I know all you want is to sleep in my room."

The kitten looked up at Katie and purred.

"Worst of all," said Katie, tickling his ears, "I still can't think of a name for you!"

That night, Katie's mother put the kitten's basket into the living room.

Katie woke up to sound of her mother shouting. Quick as a flash, she
raced downstairs.
"Oh no, little kitten!" she cried. "What have you done now?"

All over the sofa were rips and tears, and little kitten claw marks. It was ruined.
"Right!" said Katie's father. "From now on, that kitten is sleeping in the kitchen
by the back door."
"But Dad," cried Katie, "why can't he just sleep in my room? He won't cause any
trouble, I promise!"

But Katie's parents were in no mood to listen, and so the kitten's basket was
moved to the kitchen.

Trouble

The next morning, Katie rushed downstairs to check on the little kitten. "Oh no!" she cried, gazing around the kitchen in horror. It looked like an elephant had been let loose. There was food and mess everywhere!

Katie's parents were annoyed at the mess, but concerned, too. "How much trouble can one little kitten cause?" said Mother, picking up the remains of Dad's newspaper. "If he doesn't start behaving himself, we may have to think about finding a new home for him."

"Please don't send him away!" cried Katie. "I think he's just lonely. If you let him sleep in my room, I'm sure he'll be as good as gold."

"It's worth a try," said Katie's dad. "But just for tonight. If he makes any mess, or keeps us awake, then I'm afraid he'll have to go."

So that night, the kitten's basket was put in Katie's room. And before they went to sleep Katie talked sternly to the kitten.

"You must try your very hardest to be good tonight," she told him, "otherwise you will be in real trouble." She also promised him that if he was good, then she would definitely think of a name for him in the morning. The kitten just looked at her and purred, but Katie was sure that he had understood.

In the morning, her mother opened Katie's bedroom door very gingerly. "Goodness me!" she exclaimed.

Katie and the kitten were on the bed playing – and there wasn't a single sign of a mess.

"He was as good as gold all night," cried Katie. "Can he stay?"

"Of course," her mother said with a smile, "as long as he behaves and keeps out of trouble."

"That's it!" said Katie with a huge grin on her face. "That's the perfect name for him. I'll call him Trouble!"

Wilfred Wolfred

Wilfred Wolfred was a Big Bad Wolf. Well, he used to be until he turned over a new leaf and became a medium-sized good wolf instead. Wilfred Wolfred was having a Big Bad Day.

It all started when he got out of bed and stubbed his toe on the table leg. It got worse when he went to make toast and found the bread was stale. And then it got worse and worse. By mid-morning he had lost his handkerchief when he went out for a walk. And by lunchtime he had torn a hole in his best shirt!

Wilfred wondered what he had done to deserve such bad luck, especially since he had been good all week long . . .

On Monday he heard that Mrs. Red Riding Hood was having trouble with her plumbing. So, now that he was a good wolf, he gathered his tools and went to help her.

"I'm so glad to see you!" cried Mrs. Red Riding Hood. "There's a hole under my sink and the water is flooding my kitchen."

Wilfred Wolfred took his tools and after much huffing and muttering he managed to mend the hole in the pipe. All his huffing made Mrs. Red Riding Hood's daughter a little nervous, for she didn't know that Wilfred Wolfred was now a good wolf. But Wilfred barely thought about gobbling her up at all as he was so busy under the sink.

Wilfred Wolfred

On Tuesday he'd promised to help Mrs. Little Pig repair her roof. He tried not to puff too much as he mended the thatch on the roof, for fear of it blowing down again. Mrs. Little Pig's sons were supposed to help him, but he couldn't find them, so it took him a long time to fix the roof. Her sons were hiding from Wilfred, as they didn't know that Wilfred Wolfred was now a good wolf. But Wilfred certainly was not going to blow the roof down again after his work to fix it.

On Wednesday he got a phone call from Mrs. Goat. Her grandfather clock was going wrong and kept chiming all the time and waking her kids up. Now Wilfred was feeling rather tired, but since he was now a good wolf he forced himself out of bed and went to help. Luckily it was only a white mouse that was stuck inside it, so he didn't have to stay too long. This was a great relief for the seven little goats, as they were sure that Wilfred Wolfred was going to gobble them up. But Wilfred was too busy stopping himself from thinking how the mouse might make a tasty mid-morning snack to worry about them.

Wilfred Wolfred

On Thursday he went for a walk. As he passed underneath a very tall tree he heard cries. Stuck at the top of the tree was The Boy Who Cried Wolf. Even though he was very hungry and wasn't at all sure the boy was really stuck, Wilfred climbed up to help. And though his mouth watered, and he could have easily gobbled up the boy without anyone noticing, he didn't.

Now, here he was on Friday having a Big Bad Day. He'd done nothing but good deeds all week, and yet he was having the worst luck. He felt very annoyed. What was the point of being good if bad things happened to him?

Wilfred Wolfred

"Maybe if I go back to being bad, good things will happen to me?" he thought to himself. And that's exactly what he set out to do!

First of all he decided to pay Mrs. Red Riding Hood a visit. When he peeked through the window he saw that she was busy taking something out of the stove, so he crept around the other side, where he saw Little Red Riding Hood. She was all by herself in the garden.

So he crept behind the bush, and was just about to pounce, when . . .
"Ah, Wilfred Wolfred, the very wolf I wanted to see!" came a voice
Wilfred stood up quickly, looking sheepish. Well, wolfish.
"Oh, good afternoon, Mrs. Red Riding Hood," he replied.
"I was just coming to find you. I've made you a chocolate cake to thank you for helping me mend my leaky sink," she said.

So Wilfred wolfed down a huge piece of the cake and thanked
Mrs. Red Riding Hood.

"Lucky I didn't eat her daughter," he thought to himself. As after all, there is nothing more delicious than chocolate cake.

Wilfred Wolfred

Even though a nice thing had happened to him, Wilfred still felt he should do something big and bad. After all, he had changed back now. So he decided to pay a visit to the Little Pigs' house.

Mrs. Little Pig was inside the house sewing. While she wasn't looking he crept into the garden where the three tasty brothers were sleeping in the sunshine. His mouth watering, he was just about to pounce, when . . .

"Ah, Wilfred Wolfred, the very wolf I wanted to see!" came a voice.

Wilfred stood up quickly, looking very red-faced.
"Oh, good afternoon Mrs. Little Pig" he replied.
"I was just coming to find you, to see if you needed any sewing done and to thank you for helping me fix my roof," she said.

So Wilfred went to get his best shirt with the hole in it, and thought how lucky it was that he hadn't gobbled up her sons, or his shirt would never have been mended.

After that he decided to pay a visit to Mrs. Goat.

He was just on his was way when . . .

"Wilfred Wolfred!" shouted a voice. It was the Boy Who Cried Wolf, running towards him.
"Oh, here comes a tasty snack," thought Wilfred, "I get to be bad at last!"
He was just about to pounce, when he saw something. The Boy Who Cried Wolf was holding his handkerchief.
"I saw it from the top of the tree," he panted. "I wanted to return it as a thank you for saving me."

Wilfred Wolfred

Wilfred Wolfred thanked the boy, for he was very fond of that handkerchief. He was just about to set out again to Mrs. Goat's house to be really big and bad, when he thought about all the nice things that had happened that day. His tummy was full of chocolate cake. His best shirt had been mended, and his handkerchief had been returned. And his toe hardly hurt at all any more. His big bad day was actually turning out rather well. And it wasn't because he had done anything big and bad, it was because of the good things he had done.

So, then and there, he decided to turn back into a Big Good Wolf. And he would never think about gobbling anyone up ever again. Well, hardly ever.

The Golden Goose

Once upon a time, there were three brothers. The two older brothers were clever and strong, but the youngest was small and shy. The rest of the family teased him and called him names.

One day, their father told them he needed some wood from the forest for the fire. The oldest and strongest brother jumped up.

"Father, let me go," he said. "I am the strongest and the smartest. I will go into the forest and bring back more wood than you'll ever need!"

So his mother gave the brother a loaf of freshly baked bread and a bottle of good wine. "Take these," she told him. "You will need something to nourish you and quench your thirst."

When the oldest brother reached the forest, he met an old man.

"Good day to you, young sir," called the old man. "I am famished. Do you have any bread?"

"Yes," replied the brother, "but I need it for my own lunch. I cannot spare any."

"In that case," said the man, "do you have anything to drink? I have had nothing all day!"

"I'm sorry," said the brother. "I would give you some wine, but I need it for myself. Chopping wood is thirsty work. Now, if you don't mind, I'm very busy, so I must be on my way!"

"It is a shame you cannot spare anything for me. Remember this if something happens to you," replied the old man mysteriously.

The oldest brother marched off into the forest and found a fine tree to chop. He had not been working long when CHIP! CHOP! OUCH! His hand slipped, and the axe cut him.

"Oh! Oh! My poor finger!" he cried. And he picked up his axe and ran home, wondering all the way if the strange old man had something to do with the accident.

The next day, the second brother went to his father.

"Father," he said, "I feel it is my duty as your second-born son to take up the work my poor injured brother could not finish yesterday." So he too was given a lunch of fresh bread and wine, and off he went to the forest to chop wood.

When he reached the forest, the second brother met the same old man.

"Good day to you, young sir," smiled the old man. "Could you spare some of your lunch for a hungry old man?"

The second brother thought for a second. "I do have some bread," he replied, "but I surely cannot spare any, for I don't want to starve myself!"

"Then maybe a little of your wine to ease my thirst?" asked the old man.

"If you drink it, what shall I have when I am thirsty from chopping wood?" replied the second brother. "I'm sorry. You'll have to find some of your own. Now, if you will excuse me, I have work to do."

"It is a shame you cannot spare anything for me. Remember this if something should happen to you," the old man replied . . .

With that, the brother marched off into the forest, and began work. CHIP! CHOP! OUCH! The axe slipped and struck him on the foot. He let out a howl and he cursed the strange little man, for he was sure that this accident was his doing. Then he hopped all the way home!

31

The Golden Goose

The next day, the youngest of the three brothers went to his father.
"Let me go to chop wood for the fire," he said. "My brothers are in no state to work, and so it falls to me to finish the job."

The older brothers mocked their younger sibling, and laughed that he would be too weak to chop the wood. But the family needed the wood, and so the youngest brother was sent on his way. There was no fresh bread left, and his older brothers had drunk all the wine, so all he was given was a piece of stale crust, and a flask of water from the well.

When the youngest brother reached the edge of the forest, he too met the little old man.
"Would you share your lunch with me?" the old man asked the boy.
"I only have stale old bread and water," replied the youngest brother, "but you are welcome to share it."

The old man thanked him. And when the boy took out the bread, it was as fresh as the morning it had been baked. What was more, the water had turned into sweet wine.

As they sat and ate, the old man turned to the boy. "Because you have been kind to me, I will tell you a secret," he said, pointing to an old, withered tree. "Chop down that tree, and you will find something underneath it."

So the youngest of the brothers took the axe and swung at the old tree until it fell.

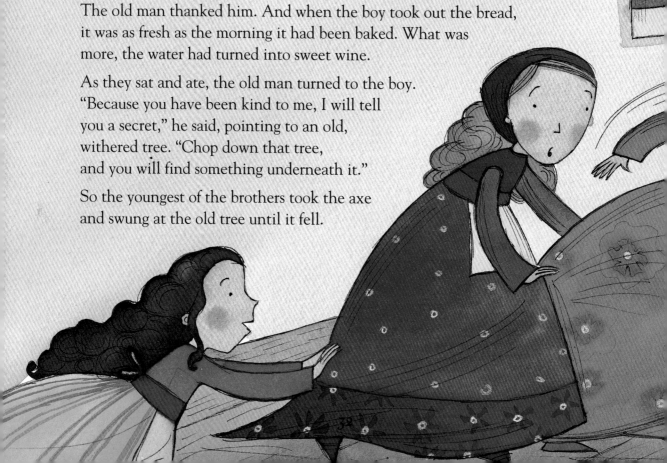

There, sitting among the roots, was a goose with feathers of pure gold.

The youngest brother knew that if he returned home, the goose would be taken away from him, so he found an inn where he could stay. The innkeeper had three daughters, and when they saw the goose, each one secretly decided they would wait for the right moment and then pluck one of the golden feathers.

Later that evening, when the boy was sleeping, the eldest of the daughters crept into his room and seized the goose. But when she tried to pull her hand away, she found that she could not remove a single feather. She was stuck fast!

Next came the second daughter, looking for a feather to pinch. But the very moment she touched her sister, she also became stuck!

The third sister came in soon after, and thought she had chanced upon a game the other girls were playing. She ran to her sisters, and before they had time to warn her, she too was completely stuck!

The next morning, the boy awoke to find the innkeeper's three daughters attached to the golden goose. To teach them a lesson, he picked up the goose and marched right out of the door, so that the daughters had to follow him wherever he decided to go.

As he marched them through the streets of the village, they passed the church. "Dear me," cried the priest, who was standing outside. "What a shameful thing it is to see three girls chasing some poor boy through our little village. Let go of him, I beg you." And he reached out to pull at the youngest daughter's sleeve as they passed by.

But as the priest grabbed hold of her, he too became stuck fast by the goose's magic, and so was forced to run behind them.

The youngest son led the procession out of the village and into the fields, where they passed two farmers.

When the priest saw these big, strong men, he called out to them. "Please help! I'm stuck! Perhaps the two of you could pull me free?"

So the farmers ran over and took hold of the priest. But as soon as they did so, they too became fixed and had to follow wherever they were led.

Soon the boy reached the city. The King who ruled the city had a beautiful daughter who was very sad. No one could cheer her up. In desperation, the King had put forth an order saying that any man who could make his daughter happy could have her hand in marriage.

As soon as the youngest of the brothers heard this, he went directly to the royal court, followed by the innkeeper's three daughters, the priest and the two farmers, of course.

When the King's daughter witnessed this strange procession, she immediately burst into peals of laughter! The King, however, did not like the look of this silly boy and his goose, and changed his mind about the promise he had made.
"You can only marry my daughter if you bring him a man who can eat a mountain of bread," he told him.

So the boy went back to the forest where he had first found the goose. There he found the little old man, sitting on a tree stump, as before.
"I am so hungry, I could eat a mountain!" cried the old man, rubbing his tummy. "Do you know where I can find more food?"
"I do," replied the boy. And he took the old man back to the royal court, where a huge mountain of bread had been baked. The old man ate and ate and ate.
By the end of the day the mountain was gone, and the old man had disappeared. Still the King was not satisfied.

"If you want to marry my daughter you must bring me a ship that can sail on land and water!" he demanded, certain this time that the boy would fail.

But the boy was wiser than he looked. "The old man has helped me twice," he thought to himself. "Why not a third time?"

So he returned to the forest to find the old man. Sure enough, he found him waiting in a clearing.

"Because you are kind and generous, I will help you one last time," said the old man. In a flash there was a huge ship with wheels and sails, standing right next to them!

The youngest brother climbed aboard and sailed the ship across fields and lakes, meadows and rivers, all the way back to the city.

When the King saw this, he couldn't believe his eyes. But he knew there was nothing he could do. Reluctantly, he agreed at last to the marriage.

And so the youngest son, who was once teased and made fun of, married a princess and became a royal prince. In time, the young couple inherited the kingdom. The brothers and parents of the youngest son begged his forgiveness for teasing him, and the son, being generous of heart, invited them to live in his kingdom. And so they all lived happily with each other for many years after.

The Adventures of Tiny Pony

Clippity clop, clippity clop, around the field Tiny Pony bounced and hopped. It was such a beautiful day; birds were singing in the trees and poppies danced in the gentle breeze, but Tiny Pony was bored. He longed for excitement. He wanted to go on an adventure! But first he needed to find someone to go on an adventure with.

So Tiny Pony bounced and hopped over to the orchard, where Billy Goat was busy clearing up the fallen apples that lay around the ground.
"Billy Goat, Billy Goat," said Tiny Pony, "let's go off on an adventure!"
"Hmmm," said Billy Goat, munching away on the juicy red fruit, "what kind of adventure did you have in mind?"

"Well," said Tiny Pony, "I was thinking that we might fight a dragon."

But Billy Goat just snorted scornfully and said, "A little thing like you against a huge, fire-breathing dragon? You'd be roasted in seconds! Tiny ponies are not supposed to have adventures. Anyway I'm having a big enough adventure right here eating all these apples."

And with that he turned his back to keep crunching and munching.

But this didn't change Tiny Pony's mind. Maybe he wouldn't be much good at fighting dragons, but that didn't mean he couldn't have a different kind of adventure.

So Tiny Pony bounced and hopped over to the meadow, where Dylan the sheepdog was busy rounding up the sheep.

"Dylan, Dylan, let's go on an adventure!"

"Hmm," said Dylan the sheepdog, "what kind of adventure were you thinking of?"

"Well," said Tiny Pony, "I was thinking that we might rescue a princess from a very tall tower."

But Dylan the sheepdog howled with laughter. "You're not a handsome prince. A princess would send you away in seconds. Anyway, I'm having a big enough adventure right here, rounding up sheep."

And with that he turned his back to keep herding his flock.

But this didn't change Tiny Pony's mind. Maybe Dylan was right, but that didn't mean he couldn't have a different kind of adventure. So Tiny Pony clipped and clopped over to the farmyard, where Paisley the pig was rolling in the mud of her messy sty.

"Paisley, Paisley," said Tiny Pony, "let's go off on an adventure!"
"What kind of adventure were you thinking of?" yawned Paisley the pig.
"Well," said Tiny Pony, "I was thinking that we might find some treasure at the top of a beanstalk."

But Paisley the pig just grunted a lazy grunt. "Have you forgotten that there are giants at the top of beanstalks? Anyway, I'm having a big enough adventure right here in this mud."

And with that she turned her back and buried herself deeper in the sty.

"Well," sighed Tiny Pony to himself, "if I can't fight dragons, rescue princesses or climb beanstalks, what kind of adventure can I have?"

Just then, a huge black cloud floated to where the sun had been shining. Big drops of rain started to fall from the sky. Then a fierce wind whipped through the trees, flattening the poppies against the ground.
"Help!" yelled a voice from the orchard.

Tiny Pony ran as fast as he could back to the orchard. Billy Goat was running around trying to catch all the apples that the wind was blowing from the trees. "If all the apples fall to the ground they'll be ruined," wailed Billy Goat, "and the farmer won't have a crop!"

"Don't worry, I have an idea," cried Tiny Pony, and off he trotted to his stable to fetch the huge basket the farmer used for storing hay. Clutching the basket between his teeth, Tiny Pony bounced all around the orchard, and the apples plop-plop-plopped into the basket of hay until it was full. Not one of them was bruised!

Then, as suddenly as it had started, the storm died down again. Tiny Pony was about to go back to thinking of adventures when he heard a loud howling.

"Help!" howled a voice from the meadow.

Tiny Pony clip-clopped as fast as he could to the meadow. Dylan the sheepdog was running in and out of the long grass.

"The storm has frightened my sheep," said Dylan, "and now one of them has run away."

"Don't worry, I have an idea," said Tiny Pony, and he galloped to the top of the hill, from where he could see the entire farm. There was no sign of a stray sheep anywhere in the meadow, the orchard, or the farmyard. But there, over by the barn, Tiny Pony could just see a little shivering sheep's tail sticking out from beneath the tractor.

Quick as a flash, Tiny pony galloped back to tell Dylan where his lost sheep could be found.

The Adventures of Tiny Pony

Tiny Pony was just about to go back to thinking of adventures again when he heard an almighty shriek.

"Help!" squealed a voice from the pig sty.

Tiny Pony ran as fast as he could over to the meadow. There he saw Paisley the pig in a mountain of mud.

"The storm made all this new mud, and I was so happy I buried myself as deep as can be, but now the sun has dried it up and I'm stuck fast."

"Don't worry, I have an idea," said Tiny Pony, and he immediately began using his clippety hooves to break away the baked mud. With each clip and clop a chunk of mud went flying across the farmyard, until finally Paisley was free.

Tiny Pony lay in his field feeling exhausted but not even a little bit bored when Billy Goat, Dylan the sheepdog and Paisley the pig came to join him.

"We've been thinking," said Billy Goat, "and we've decided that while some tiny ponies are not supposed to have adventures, you certainly are. So maybe we should all leave the farm and go off to find one."

Tiny Pony was about to ask his friends what kind of adventure they had in mind, when he was suddenly struck with a thought.
"It's very kind of you all," he said, "but I think there are more than enough adventures right here on this farm."

The Elves & the Shoemaker

Once there was a shoe shop that sold the most fabulous shoes. People came from far and wide to buy shoes from this shop; it was world famous!

But the shoemaker had not always been so successful. In fact, he had once been so poor he had lost almost everything he owned and had just enough material left to make one last pair of shoes!

He laid out his tools and leather ready for the morning and said to his wife, "To-morrow I shall make my last pair of shoes and then what will we do?"
"Do not worry, my dear," said his wife. "We are good people. We shall find a way."

When the shoemaker awoke the very next morning, he couldn't believe his eyes. Sitting on his workbench was a beautiful pair of shoes!

He looked closer and saw that the shoes were put together perfectly, with every single stitch in the right place! The shoemaker and his wife didn't know what to think, but before they had time to figure it out, there was a knock at the door.

47

The shoemaker opened it to see a man standing outside.
"I am sorry for calling so early," said the man, "but I have been on the road all night and my shoes are worn out! I don't suppose you have a new pair you could sell me?"

So the shoemaker showed the customer the brand-new pair of shoes.

The customer loved them and they fitted him perfectly! He paid the shoemaker a handsome price for the shoes.

With the money he had earned, the shoemaker went out and bought the materials he needed to make two more pairs of shoes.

That evening the shoemaker laid out all his work again, as he had done the night before. Once again when he woke the next morning, there, sitting on the workbench, were two brand-new pairs of shoes!

The shoemaker and his wife were astonished! Who on earth could have made these wonderful shoes?

Then once again they heard a knock at the door. They opened it to two men. "Please excuse us for our rudeness," they said. "Our good friend visited us yesterday wearing what could only be described as the most glorious shoes we have ever seen! We simply had to come and see for ourselves the shop that sells these shoes! And would you perhaps have any for sale?"

So the shoemaker showed the customers in. They tried on the new shoes, and once again they fitted perfectly. This time the customers paid double!
The shoemaker once again bought materials and got everything ready for the next day's work. Once more the shoes were all completed when he awoke and there were even more customers already waiting outside the shop!
Every shoe fitted every foot perfectly, even though they were all different.

The shoemaker made enough extra money to buy a wonderful meal for his wife along with the materials for the next day.

Just before they went to bed the shoemaker's wife said, "My darling, we have been ever so fortunate to be blessed by whatever magic has made these shoes. Let us stay awake and watch what happens, and then maybe we can somehow thank whoever has been helping us."

So the shoemaker and his wife stayed up and hid behind a big armchair in the corner of the room. They waited and waited and then suddenly, when the clock struck midnight, a dozen little elves came tumbling down the chimney!

They watched in amazement as the elves picked up the tools and the leather and began making the shoes.

When all the work was done the elves bounced back up the chimney leaving behind some of the finest footwear the shoemaker had ever seen!

"We must do something for these elves," said the shoemaker's wife. "They have surely saved our little shoe shop. There must be some way to repay them!"

The shoemaker thought about it for a moment then said, "Did you see their feet?"
"Yes!" replied his wife. "They weren't wearing any shoes!"
"Perhaps I could make them new pairs of shoes?" said the shoemaker.
"Yes! That's a wonderful idea!" said the shoemaker's wife.
"And did you see those tatty old rags they were wearing? Well, I shall make them some beautiful new clothes to wear instead."

So that very day the shoemaker began making twelve little pairs of shoes while his wife made twelve fine shirts and twelve pairs of trousers.

That evening, when the shoemaker laid out his materials for the next day, he also left out twelve tiny outfits and twelve tiny pairs of shoes. The shoemaker and his wife hid behind the big armchair again and waited for the elves to appear.

When midnight arrived, the elves came tumbling down the chimney again and saw the beautiful presents that had been left for them.

The elves were ecstatic! They cheered and danced and then put on their new shoes and one by one they jumped out of the window. The shoemaker never saw the elves again, but he continued to make beautiful shoes using the secret tricks he learned from watching them. The shoemaker went on to be very successful and his shoes became well known in all the fashionable cities.

The Magic Dancing Shoes

Annabel wanted nothing more than to be able to dance. Her grandmother had been a very famous dancer, and Annabel would spend hours looking at all the old photographs and trophies at her grandparents' house. She would imagine herself on stage, in the spotlight, dancing in front of a huge crowd.

But no matter how hard she tried, Annabel couldn't make her feet do what she wanted them to. She watched enviously as the other girls in her class twirled across the floor. "Why am I so clumsy?" she would sigh.

One day, Annabel was visiting her grandparents' house, when her grandma took her aside. "How are the dancing lessons going, Annabel?" she asked.
"Oh Nana, I just can't do it!" cried Annabel. "I'm always practicing, but I just can't get it right."
"Of course you can!" laughed her grandmother. "You just have to believe you can do it. Now wait there a moment. I have something for you."

Nana came back with a cardboard box and handed it to Annabel.
"Well, open it!" she laughed.

Inside the box, hidden beneath crumpled brown paper, was the prettiest, most delicate music box Annabel had ever seen. She opened it to find a little fairy ballerina spinning around to a simple, elegant melody.
"It's beautiful Nana! Thank you!" cried Annabel.

"It belonged to me when I was a little girl," said Nana. "You must promise to take very good care of it. That music box is much more special than you think."

Annabel wasn't really sure what she meant by this, but she gave her a big hug and then ran off to show her parents the wonderful gift.

When they got home, Annabel went straight
up to her room and wound up the music box.
She watched as the fairy ballerina twirled
around and around.

"How I wish I could dance like you!"
Annabel sighed. As she spoke, there was
a flash. Before Annabel's startled eyes, the
fairy ballerina in the box yawned, stretched
her arms, then fluttered into the air, before
coming to rest lightly on Annabel's bed.
"Thank you, Annabel," said the fairy
ballerina in a tiny voice. "It feels so good
to be out of that box at last! Now I would
like to do something for you. When you wake
up in the morning, you will find a pair of
dancing shoes at the foot of your bed.
Put them on and you shall become the
greatest dancer in the world!"

Without another word, the fairy flew into the air and out of the open window. Annabel could hardly believe what she had seen.

"My imagination must be playing tricks on me," she thought, as she climbed into bed that night. She knew that fairies didn't really exist. And as for a pair of magic shoes that could make you dance – she had never heard such a ridiculous idea!

All through the night the little ballerina danced through Annabel's dreams. And when Annabel woke up, she couldn't resist checking at the foot of her bed . . . even though she was sure there would be nothing there.

But to her astonishment, she found a pair of beautiful dancing shoes, just as the fairy ballerina had promised!

The shoes didn't look very magical, but Annabel couldn't wait to see if they would really work. She slipped them on her feet and stood in the middle of her room, ready to attempt a pirouette. Before she had a chance even to think about what she was doing, she found herself spinning around on the tips of her toes like a real ballerina. She could dance! Unable to believe it, Annabel tried the other steps she had learned in class. She performed them all perfectly.

"What will Miss Carr say?" she giggled, as she spun round and round.

Annabel's dance teacher, Miss Carr, was very impressed with her progress. "You have been working hard, Annabel!" she said at the next class.

"Yes," replied Annabel, smiling to herself. "My nana helped me."

Later that term, Miss Carr took Annabel aside at the end of the lesson. "I think you are ready to take on one of the lead roles in the show at the end of term," she said. "Would you like to?"

Annabel was overjoyed. "Oh yes!" she cried. "Thank you so much!"

Then she ran off to tell her mother and father the wonderful news.

The following week, Miss Carr announced the show in class. There were mutters of disapproval from some of the older girls when they found out Annabel had the lead role. But Annabel tried not to care what the others thought. She just wanted to dance! So she worked as hard as she could to learn all the new steps for the show. Of course, the magic shoes made it a lot easier – but Annabel still worked harder than ever before. She wanted every single step to be perfect.

Finally, the day of the show came. Annabel felt nervous and excited all at once. Her parents were coming to watch. Most importantly, Nana would be there, sitting in the front row. Annabel waited in the wings, listening to the auditorium filling up.

She couldn't believe she was going to dance in front of all these people.

"Hurry up Annabel," called Miss Carr, interrupting her thoughts. "It's time to finish getting ready for the show."

Annabel rushed off to the dressing room to find her magic dancing shoes. But when she got there the shoes were gone! What on earth would she do? How would she ever dance as well as she had with the magic shoes?

Annabel felt tears welling up in her eyes. There was no way she could do the show now! How would she explain herself?

As she sat by herself, wondering what to do, Annabel suddenly felt the tiniest tap on her shoulder. Then there was a little whisper in her ear.
"It's the big show, Annabel! Why are you sitting here crying?"

She rubbed her eyes and looked up to see the fairy ballerina spinning excitedly.
"I've been watching you, Annabel, and you really are an amazing dancer." she said.
"But my magic shoes are gone!" cried Annabel. "I can't dance without them."

The fairy looked over at her and smiled.
"The shoes weren't really magic, Annabel!" she said. "The dancing was inside you all along. All you have to do is believe in yourself, and you will find that your heart knows every step."
Annabel was shocked. Had it really been her dancing all this time, and not the shoes? Maybe she could do the show after all.

Annabel hurried to find Miss Carr, and together they went to find a spare pair of dancing shoes in the store wardrobe. Annabel put them on and made her way nervously to the stage. She stood behind the great big curtain, closed her eyes and breathed in deeply. The curtain rose slowly, and the music began.

From then on, the evening turned into a blur of spinning, jumping and swirling light and sound. Annabel was lost in the music and dancing.

When the curtain finally came down, Annabel was in a daze. She got changed and went to meet her parents and grandparents at the stage door. Everyone told her how amazing she had been.

"I've never seen you dance better, Annabel," said Nana, giving her a hug. "I'm so proud of you." Then she took her hand and whispered in her ear, "Don't worry, the fairy told me what happened. We'll get you a new pair of dancing shoes for those magic feet of yours!"

Annabel could only stare in amazement as her grandmother put a finger to her lips. "And if you keep it a secret," she whispered, "I'll even teach you some new steps!"

Little Red Hen

L ittle Red Hen was pecking and clucking in the farmyard when,
all of a sudden, she came upon a grain of wheat.
"I could eat this wheat," she said to her friends, "or we could plant it in the
ground and then maybe it will grow and feed us all."

And so she asked, "Who will help me plant this grain?"
"Not I," quacked the duck.
"Not I," honked the goose.
"Not I," mewed the cat.
"Very well," said Little Red Hen. "Then I shall plant the grain."
And so she made a little hole in a clearing and planted the grain all by herself.

The very next day, Little Red Hen looked at the spot where she had planted the grain and saw that it was dry. And so she asked her friends, "Who will help me water this grain?"

"Not I," quacked the duck.

"Not I," honked the goose.

"Not I," mewed the cat.

"Very well," said Little Red Hen. "Then I shall water the grain."

And so she brought a watering can and gave the grain a cool drink. And she did the same the next day, and the day after that, all by herself.

Very soon, the grain had grown into tall, ripe wheat, good enough to eat.

So Little Red Hen asked her friends, "Who will help me cut this wheat?"

"Not I," quacked the duck.

"Not I," honked the goose.

"Not I," mewed the cat.

"Very well," said Little Red Hen. "Then I shall cut the wheat."

And so she brought a scythe to cut the wheat and then she gathered it all up, all by herself.

Little Red Hen

Now the wheat was ready to be ground into flour, so she asked her friends, "Who will help me take this wheat to the miller?"

"Not I," quacked the duck.

"Not I," honked the goose.

"Not I," mewed the cat.

"Very well," said Little Red Hen. "Then I shall take the wheat to the miller."

And so she put the wheat on the cart, and she drove the cart to the mill.

The miller saw that the wheat was very good indeed, and there was enough to make a whole sack of flour, which Little Red Hen took back to the farm all by herself.

Now the flour was ready to be baked into bread. So Little Red Hen asked her friends, "Who will help me bake the bread?"

"Not I," quacked the duck.

"Not I," honked the goose.

"Not I," mewed the cat.

"Very well," said Little Red Hen. "Then I shall bake the bread." And so she kneaded the dough and put it into the oven. When it smelled good and ready, she asked her friends, "Who will help me eat this bread?"

"I will," quacked the duck.

"I will," honked the goose.

"I will," mewed the cat.

"Hmmm," said Little Red Hen. "No one would help me plant the grain, water it, cut the wheat, take it to the miller or bake the flour into bread. But everyone will eat it?" she asked.

"Yes," quacked the duck.

"Yes," honked the goose.

"Yes," mewed the cat.

"I don't think so," said Little Red Hen, and she ate up the bread – all by herself.

Snowfall the Unicorn

Far away, where the mountains meet the sea, there is a kingdom of great beauty. Mountains glisten with snowy tops and rivers cascade through green meadows filled with wild flowers. Neither man nor beast wants for anything.

But this was not always so. One year, springtime didn't bring the usual rains, and by summer the air was heavy with heat. It grew hotter and hotter, and the earth became cracked and parched. There was no harvest that year.

By late autumn, the King called together his most trusted advisors to discuss what could be done.

"My wise men, what suggestions do you have," asked the King, "for I fear my people will starve."

"A rain dance perhaps, your majesty? Maybe we have upset the gods," answered one advisor. The dancer was summoned, but no rains came.

The King once again called together his advisors.

"My wise men, what shall we do?" the king asked.

"Our food stocks are almost empty and my people are thirsty."

"Your majesty we could divert the great river from the north of the kingdom to provide water for everyone," suggested another.

So they journeyed to the north, but when they arrived the great river had dried up and disappeared.

69

Winter came, yet the terrible heat continued. Many of the people bade farewell to their homes and set off to other kingdoms in search of food and water.

On Christmas Eve, Princess Natasha, the King's youngest daughter, gazed sadly out of her bedroom window. In the moonlight she could see the dry and parched kingdom. Tears ran down her cheeks as she looked at the wretched landscape. "Will we ever see snow again?" she whispered to herself. "If only I could do something to save the kingdom. But what can a little girl like me do? Princess Natasha glanced up into the evening sky, where a lone star was twinkling. "Please, bring back the snow," she whispered.

The star twinkled even more brightly. Again she pleaded with the star, "Please, bring back the snow to our poor kingdom."

The star twinkled at her once more, and seemed to move. So Natasha put on her cloak and decided to follow it. She didn't know what else she could do.

The princess followed the bright star. She walked for hours through the dusty fields until she came to the dried-up forest. There, in the middle of a clearing, surrounded by withered trees, she found a unicorn bound with thick rope.

"You poor creature!" she cried, kneeling beside the beast. "Who could have done such a thing?"

The unicorn was very still, but when Natasha stroked its back it opened its eyes and looked at her sadly.

"Don't worry," said Princess Natasha.

"I shall help you."

And she set about loosening the ropes, until eventually the unicorn was free.

Snowfall the Unicorn

As the magical creature rose from the ground something caught Natasha's eye: a tiny white speck floated down from the sky and landed gently on her nose. It was a snowflake!

Soon snowflakes were swirling all around them.
"Thank you, Princess Natasha," said the unicorn. "My name is Snowfall. I control the seasons and bring the winter snow, but I was captured by a band of hunters who tied me up. Unless I am free I have no magical powers."

The snow continued to fall all around them as the unicorn knelt before the princess and offered his back to take her home. And as they rode through the forest something magical happened. With each step they took the trees started to turn green and the grass sprang from the earth once more. Soon the air was filled with the sound of birdsong and forest creatures scurried among the growing hedgerows.

Finally they reached the King's castle, bringing with them the beautiful snow. It was the best Christmas gift anyone could ever ask for. When the King heard what had happened he begged Snowfall to stay at the palace so they could keep him safe. And so it came to be that the unicorn lived in the castle garden, and Natasha visited him every day.

Ever since that time, the long summer days are once again filled with bright sunshine, and when winter comes the land is always covered in a blanket of pure white snow. And every Christmas the people look up at the stars twinkling above them, and it reminds them of the terrible year when the unicorn was captured. And they give thanks to the beautiful creature who once again roams free.

Chicken Little

Chicken Little was wandering through the woods one day when PLOP, something small and hard fell onto her head. "Ouch," said Chicken Little. "That felt like the sky was falling." But the sky was not falling. What Chicken Little had felt was an acorn falling from a tree, although she didn't know that.

On through the woods went Chicken Little when PLOP, something else fell on her head. "Ouch," she cried. "That really, really felt like the sky was falling." But of course, it was another acorn falling from a tree, although Chicken Little didn't know that.

She kept on walking when PLOP! PLOP! PLOP! Three acorns fell on her head all at once. "Help!" yelled Chicken Little. "The sky really is falling!"

As she was rushing along, she bumped into Henny Penny, who was out for
a stroll.
"Help!" said Chicken Little to Henny Penny, "the sky is falling!" "Where?" asked
Henny Penny, looking around in shock.
"Right on my head," said Chicken Little. "We must go to tell the King."
So, Chicken Little and Henny Penny set out to tell the King.

On the way, they met Ducky Lucky, who was going to the pond.
"Help!" said Henny Penny to Ducky Lucky. "The sky is falling!"
"Where?" asked Ducky Lucky, looking around in shock.
"Right on Chicken Little's head," said Henny Penny. "We must go to tell the
King." So Chicken Little, Henny Penny and Ducky Lucky set out to tell
the King.

On the way, they met Cocky Locky, who was going to the barnyard.
"Help!" said Ducky Lucky to Cocky Locky. "The sky is falling!"
"Where?" asked Cocky Locky, looking around in shock.
"Right on Chicken Little's head," said Ducky Lucky. "We must go to tell the
King." So Chicken Little, Henny Penny, Ducky Lucky and Cocky Locky set out
to tell the king.

Chicken Little

On the way, they met Goosey Lucy, who was going to the market.
"Help!" said Cocky Locky to Goosey Lucy. "The sky is falling!"
"Where?" asked Goosey Lucy, looking around in shock.
"Right on Chicken Little's head," said Cocky Locky. "We must go to tell the King." So Chicken Little, Henny Penny, Ducky Lucky, Cocky Locky and Goosey Lucy set out to tell the King.

On the way, they met Turkey Lurkey, who was going to the meadow.
"Help!" said Goosey Lucy to Turkey Lurkey. "The sky is falling!"
"Where?" asked Turkey Lurkey, looking around in shock.
"Right on Chicken Little's head," said Goosey Lucy. "We must go to tell the King." So Chicken Little, Henny Penny, Ducky Lucky, Cocky Locky, Goosey Lucy and Turkey Lurkey set out to tell the King.

Chicken Little

On the way, they met Foxy Loxy, who was going to his den.
"Help!" said Turkey Lurkey to Foxy Loxy. "The sky is falling!"
Where?" asked Foxy Loxy, looking around in shock.
"Right on Chicken Little's head," said Turkey Lurkey. "We must go tell the King."

But Foxy Loxy said that if the sky was falling, they would be safer waiting in his den until the danger was over. So Chicken Little, Henny Penny, Ducky Lucky, Cocky Locky, Goosey Lucy and Turkey Lurkey all followed Foxy Loxy into his den.

But of course it was not safe in the den and the danger was far from over, for Foxy Loxy gobbled up Chicken Little, Henny Penny, Ducky Lucky, Cocky Locky, Goosey Lucy and Turkey Lurkey. And the King never did find out that the sky was falling.

Treasure Island

Z oe and Amy lived with their mother and father and a puppy called Jake in a white cottage overlooking the sea, with a path of crushed shells that ran down to a rocky beach below.

The two girls loved swimming, and spent almost all their spare time on the beach, or in the water. They practically lived in their bathing suits or wetsuits, and had earned themselves the name of "The Water Babes" in their family.

One sunny afternoon, Zoe and Amy were having a picnic in the garden with their grandmother, looking out over the sea as they ate.

Suddenly, Zoe spoke. "Have you ever been to that island, Nana?" she asked, pointing to a small mound rising up out of the water off the shore.

"Oh yes," replied Nana. "But it was a very long time ago. It has a beautiful white sandy beach on the other side, where seals bask in the sunshine."

Their grandmother closed her eyes for a moment, as if remembering. Then she smiled a long slow smile. "And do you know why I was there?" she asked. "For treasure!"

"You mean there's treasure on the island?" asked Amy excitedly. "Yes," laughed their grandmother, "and I know where to find it."

All afternoon, the girls could talk of nothing but treasure, and how to get to the island. They were still talking about it at bedtime that night.

"It's too far to swim," said Zoe, as she climbed into bed and snuggled under the covers. "But we could make a raft. Let's start in the morning."

Early the next day, Zoe and Amy headed to the beach, talking excitedly.
"If we are going to make a raft," said Amy, "we need to collect things to make
it. There are some things we can use on the beach." And off they ran along the
shore, with Jake at their heels.

Before long, they had collected two worn rubber wheels, three planks of wood
and some old rope. "It might look like a pile of old junk now," laughed Amy,
"but it won't be long before we are floating over to the island."

Dad watched the two girls from the upstairs window and smiled. He went to the
local newspaper, turned the pages, then picked up the phone.
"Hello Mr. Brown," he said. "I'm calling about your For Sale ad."

The girls worked all day on their raft. But building
one that would actually float with two girls sitting
on top was much harder than they had expected.
"Let's finish it tomorrow," suggested Amy at the
end of the afternoon. "I'm too tired and
hungry to do any more."

The next morning, Zoe and Amy got up early again to work on their raft. "Look at that sign on Dad's door!" exclaimed Zoe, as they walked down the garden path past his workshop.
"Top Secret. Keep Out!" read Amy. "What do you think he's doing in there?"

There was a lot of banging and clattering going on inside the workshop, and they could hear Dad singing at the top of his voice.
"Let us in, Dad!" cried Amy, ignoring the sign. "Can we see?"

For a moment the banging stopped, and the door opened very slightly. Dad's head peeked around. "Sorry," he said. "Like the sign says, this is top secret." Then the door closed and the banging began once again.

The girls were bursting to know what Dad was up to, but he obviously wasn't going to tell them. So they headed down to the beach to finish their raft. There was treasure to be found.

During the night, an old fish crate had washed up on the shore.
"This will float," said Zoe, hauling it up the beach. Very carefully, the girls secured the rubber wheels to each side of the crate, with the wooden planks tied on like skis underneath it. Finally, Amy got their life jackets and some old oars that they found in the garage. They were ready for the launch!

"I've got a treasure map from Nana," said Amy, rolling up a sheet of paper and tucking inside her life jacket. "She drew it for me last night."
"We're about to launch the raft," shouted Zoe.
Their mother, who was in the garden, waved at the girls and walked down to the beach.
"Is there room for me, too?" she asked.
"Sure," replied Amy. "Welcome aboard."

With that, Zoe and Amy and their mother pushed the little raft into the sea. At first, the raft bobbed happily on the waves, and they began to paddle. But after just a little while, the waves began to wash over the little raft and it began to sink. Luckily, they were still close to shore where the water was shallow.

"I'm sorry girls," said their mother, as they hauled their vessel back onto the beach.
"I guess you didn't build it for three. Maybe you could try again tomorrow. Now why don't we go and have some cookies and hot chocolate to warm us up."

As Zoe, Amy and their mother walked back to the cottage they bumped into Dad. His work clothes were covered in white paint.
"What is Dad doing," asked Amy, "and why is it a secret?"
Their mother just smiled, "now what about that hot chocolate?"

That evening, Zoe and Amy felt down. The summer vacation was almost over.
"Do you think we'll manage to reach the island before we go back to school?" sighed Zoe, as they lay in bed.
"We can try!" replied Amy. "We just need to come up with a better plan."
And, with that, they turned off the light and were soon fast asleep.

The next morning, Amy was awakened by shouting from downstairs.
"Amy, come quick!" yelled Zoe. "There's a letter for us on the kitchen table."
Amy dashed downstairs. "What does it say?" she asked excitedly.
"To my darling Water Babes," read Zoe. "Go to the window and look out now. Lots of love from Dad XXX."

The girls scrambled to the window. There on the beach were their mother and father ... and a little red wooden rowing boat. Zoe and Amy had never moved so fast! Wetsuits and life jackets pulled on, they raced down to the shore.
"Where did it come from?" cried Amy, her cheeks flushed.
"From Mr. Brown," said Dad proudly. "Now she's ready for her first adventure."

The girls climbed eagerly into the little boat, then Dad launched it into the water, and jumped aboard. At last they were off to their treasure island.

Just a few minutes later, Dad was pulling the little boat up onto the shore of the island. Amy pulled out the map and studied it carefully.
"We need to find a big white rock," she said.
"I see it, I see it," shouted Zoe, running over to a large white boulder glinting in the sun. "Quick! Help me turn it over."

The rock was very heavy, but between them they rolled it away. Underneath they found a battered wooden box with a rusty catch. Zoe found a stick and jammed it under the catch. Finally, the lock sprang open.
"Wow!" the girls cried in unison. "It really is treasure!"
Inside was a gold locket, a ruby ring, a purse of coins and some photographs of Nana and her family when she was a little girl.

When they got back to the beach at home, Nana was waiting for them.
"Hello, my treasures. I see you've found it," she said. "I put that box there many years ago, when I was about your age. And since you found it, it's only right that you should keep it."

"Thank you!" cried Zoe and Amy, hugging her tightly.
"And now we must make our own treasure chest and bury it on the island. Then someone else can find it one day."

Snow White & Rose Red

Once upon a time, a poor widow lived with her two daughters. The girls were called Snow White and Rose Red. They were named after two rose trees that grew in front of their cottage – one red, and one white. They were very sweet and kind girls.

The two girls were very happy. When they weren't busy helping their mother, they played in the forest. The animals watched over them and always made sure they were safe. If they ever got lost, a kind bird or deer would lead them back to their cottage. On warm summer nights, they sometimes slept outside, beneath the moon. On cold winter nights, they warmed themselves beside the fire.

One cold winter's evening, they were sitting beside the fire when there was a knock at the door. Rose Red ran to pull it open.

"Aaaaahhhh!" she screamed. She was face to face with a big black bear.

"Do not be afraid. I won't hurt you," said the bear in a surprisingly gentle voice. "May I come in to warm myself beside your fire?"

"Please do, you poor bear!" said the widow.

And she welcomed him in.

At first, Snow White and Rose Red were afraid of the big black bear. Then, bit by bit, they became used to him. Before long, they were playing with him and having lots of fun.

For the rest of the winter, the bear was like one of the family. He slept beside the fire each night, and returned to the forest each day.

When spring arrived, the bear told the girls he had to go away. "I must guard my treasure from the wicked dwarfs who come out of their holes in the spring," he explained.

Later that day, Snow White and Rose Red were collecting firewood when they saw something dancing around a fallen tree. It was a angry-looking dwarf with a long, snow-white beard. His beard was trapped beneath the tree.
"What are you staring at?" he yelled at the girls. "Why don't you help?"

The girls pulled and pulled, but they could not free the beard.
"You useless brats," snarled the dwarf. "You're about as helpful as hole in the head. I could die before you get me out of here!"
"Don't worry," said Snow White. "I will help you."

Then she pulled her scissors out of her pocket and snipped his beard.
As soon as the dwarf was free, he grabbed a bag of gold from among the tree's roots and turned his back on the girls.
"Nasty girl, cutting off my fine beard," he hissed. And then he was gone.

Shortly afterwards, Snow White and Rose Red were walking by the brook when they saw the dwarf again. A big fish had caught hold of his beard and was pulling him into the water. The two girls caught hold of the dwarf and tried to pull him free. But it was no use. The fish was just too strong. Not knowing what else to do, Snow White pulled out her scissors and cut the beard.

"You toadstool!" screamed the dwarf once he was free. "Do you want to ruin all of my beautiful beard?" Then, without another word, he dragged a sack of pearls out of the reeds and disappeared.

A few days later, Snow White and Rose Red were walking to town when they heard someone scream. They ran towards the noise and saw that a huge eagle had grabbed the bad-tempered dwarf.
"Quick," said Rose Red. And each girl grabbed one of the dwarf's legs. They pulled and pulled until the eagle finally let go.

Snow White & Rose Red

The dwarf jumped to his feet and grabbed a bag of jewels.

"You clumsy creatures!" he snarled. "Couldn't you have been more careful? Look, my lovely coat is all torn."

He glared at the girls with fiery red eyes, and then disappeared down a hole.

By now the girls were so used to the ungrateful dwarf's bad manners that they continued to town without giving him a further thought.

Later that evening, the girls were returning home when they saw something sparkling in the moonlight. The dwarf was pulling sacks of treasure out of a hole and spreading it out on the grass. It looked so lovely that the girls stopped to stare.

"What are you staring at?" screamed the dwarf in a rage.

He didn't stop shouting at them until there was a loud growl and a black bear leaped out of the forest.

The dwarf was so scared that he didn't move an inch.

"D…d…dear Mr. Bear," he spluttered. "Don't hurt me. I'm just a skinny little dwarf. I wouldn't make much of a meal. Eat those girls instead. They are plump and juicy."

The bear paid no attention to his words. He sprung forward and cuffed the dwarf with a powerful paw. The dwarf gave a yell and fell to the ground.

Meanwhile, the two girls had run away to hide.

"Come back, Snow White and Rose Red," called the bear in a gentle voice.

"Don't be afraid. I won't hurt you."

It was their old friend, the bear.

Snow White and Rose Red ran to hug him. And when they did, the most surprising thing happened. His bearskin fell away to reveal a handsome young man, dressed from head to foot in gold.

"I am Prince Levi," he said. "That wicked dwarf stole my treasure and turned me into a bear. I was doomed to live as a bear for as long as he lived."

Snow White & Rose Red

As Snow White gazed into the prince's sea-blue eyes, her heart began
to pound. She was falling in love. Luckily, Prince Levi felt exactly the same.

Not long afterwards, there was a huge wedding. Snow White married Prince Levi
and Rose Red married his brother, Prince Sebastian. The girls and their mother
moved to the castle, and they all shared the treasure. But none of the treasure
was as dear to them as the two rose trees that grew outside the castle gates – one
red and one white.

The Missing Pony

G emma was stuck on the second level of her computer game. "You're not still playing that, are you?" said her mother, coming into her bedroom. "It's such a lovely day out. Why don't you get some fresh air instead?"

Gemma groaned. Her mother was always nagging her to get some fresh air, but the truth was that she hated going out lately because that meant walking past the empty field by the side of the house.

The field hadn't always been empty. Two months ago it had been home to Merry, a beautiful little roan pony, but a horse thief had come along one winter's night, and now the pony was gone.

Tears stung Gemma's eyes, but she refused to cry any more. She looked back at the computer screen; try as she might, she just couldn't get onto the next level, so a break might not be such a bad thing. She went down the stairs and gave a soft whistle.

In a flash of brown and white, her little terrier, Benji, came charging at her, wagging his tail furiously. A walk might cheer her up. Gemma and Benji headed to the place they always went: a smooth flat rock at the top of the hill that overlooked the town. There was hardly ever anyone around at this time of day, so she could let Benji run around freely and let her thoughts drift. And today, as usual, her thoughts drifted to Merry. She missed her little pony so much. She missed riding her and nuzzling her neck.

The Missing Pony

Gemma was lost in her thoughts when the sound of Benji yapping and tearing off down the opposite side of the hill made her snap out of it. In the distance Gemma could make out a figure coming from the woods on that side, heading towards her with Benji jumping around her feet. Benji, who didn't like strangers, never behaved this way, especially since Merry had been stolen.

As the figure got closer she saw the girl scoop the little dog into her arms. She was worried until she recognized who it was – Mary Donnolly, a girl she knew a little from school.

Although Gemma and Mary were in the same class, the girls didn't know each other very well at all. Gemma's friends all thought that Mary was a bit strange and avoided her. It was true that Mary was a little different from the other girls. She wore slightly odd clothes, and she was always on her own, reading books about plants and animals. When you did speak to her she didn't talk about ordinary things like phones or downloads, and Gemma guessed she was the sort of person who liked to be alone. Some of the other girls joked that Mary could do magic, but Gemma thought that was mean, so she always gave her a smile when they passed in the corridor.

The Missing Pony

As she walked up the hill with the runaway terrier tucked under her arm, Mary recognized Gemma as one of the popular girls at school. She was pretty, wore trendy clothes, and had a lot of friends who were also popular. But unlike the other girls, who nudged each other and whispered as Mary walked past, Gemma had always seemed kind.

As the classmates drew closer they smiled shyly, but when Mary handed over the little dog she wondered why she saw such sadness in Gemma's eyes.
"What's wrong?" she asked. "You look like you're missing something."

Gemma was startled by Mary's keen observation. "I'm thinking about my missing pony," she replied without thinking. Mary gave an understanding nod, but Gemma blushed. Why had she shared her secret with someone she hardly knew? "Bye for now," she smiled awkwardly, turning to leave.
"See you at school."

As Mary headed down the hill she was lost in thought. She could not forget the sadness in Gemma's eyes. "I must do my best to help her," she whispered.

When she got home, Mary went straight to her herb garden and picked a sprig
of sweet-smelling rosemary.

"For remembrance," she smiled, as she put it in her basket. Next she picked lucky
lavender, and a handful of dandelions puffballs. As she did this Mary thought
about the girls at school, and how surprised they'd be to know that some of the
things they whispered about her were true – sort of. She wasn't magic, of course.
But she was different; she had a special gift. She used natural remedies to cure sick
animals. And there was something else, too, which she couldn't quite explain.
When she made wishes, they sometimes came true. She knew the others at school
found her odd and shy, and this made her unpopular. But she didn't know how to
change things. And no amount of wishing for friends of her own seemed to help.
Her wishes only seemed to work for others . . .

That evening, Mary wove the rosemary and lavender into a ring around a pot,
and put the dandelions in the middle. Then she sat down to think about Gemma
and her lost pony. Mary held up the pot in the moonlight and gently blew. The
dandelion seeds drifted away on the cool night breeze as Mary made a wish.

In a nearby valley a little roan pony was falling asleep in his stall when the cool night breeze stirred him. He sniffed and began to wake up. His new owners worked him so hard that he was always so tired these days, but suddenly he felt he could shake off his exhaustion. He was restless.

He started to paw the floor, then he started to kick the door. Finally he used his hind legs to smash the door off its hinges, and he ran out into the night. There was somewhere else he was supposed to be; he remembered that now, and finally he was going home.

Gemma never knew how her beloved Merry came to be whinnying under her bedroom window that night. She never found out where he had been or who had taken him. But she didn't really care. She only cared that he was home and her heartache was over.

But there was one thing about the day her pony came home that nagged at her. When she had locked eyes with strange little Mary Donnelly on the hillside she had seen compassion and wisdom, but also something else; loneliness.

Gemma nuzzled Merry's soft, velvety nose and hugged her silky, smooth neck, then leaped up onto her newly saddled back. As they headed off towards the woods, Gemma urged Merry into a trot and called for Benji to catch up. "Come on boy," she called to the little dog. "We're off to make a new friend."

Clever Manka

There once lived two farmers – one mean but very rich, the other humble but very poor – and they were in dispute. The rich farmer had promised to give his best cow to the poor farmer in return for preparing his fields for planting, but was now refusing to pay his debt The poor farmer was forced to go the judge to solve the dispute.

Now, the judge was a good man, but he was young and sometimes a little foolish. Instead of granting the cow to the poor farmer, as would you or I, the young judge decided to set a riddle, and whoever solved the riddle could keep the cow.

"I want you to tell me this: what is the fastest thing in the world? What is the sweetest thing in the world? What is the richest?" And with that he dismissed the farmers until the following day.

The rich farmer went back to his wife, shaking his head. How on earth was he to come up with the right answers? But his wife laughed and said, "This is easy. I know the answers. The cow will be yours!" And then she set out her answers.

"Our horse is the fastest thing in the world, for when have we ever been overtaken on the roads? The sweetest thing in the world is surely our own honey – did you ever taste anything so fine? And the richest thing in the world is certainly our treasure chest – we have been saving gold and gems for 40 years, and no one can have more."

Clever Manka

Clever Manka

The rich farmer was very well pleased with his wife's answers, and went to bed that night happy.

The poor farmer had no wife to give him the answers, only a daughter, Manka. When he told the riddle to Manka, he said, "I fear that I shall lose the cow, and then what shall we do?" But Manka said, "Do not fret, Papa dear, for I shall tell you what to say."

The next morning the two farmers stood once more before the judge. The rich farmer puffed up his chest and bragged about the swiftness of his horse, the sweetness of his beehives and the wealth in his treasure chest.

The judge, though sometimes foolish, was not impressed and simply frowned at the rich farmer.

Then he asked the poor farmer to take his turn.

Nervously the poor farmer stepped forward and said, "The fastest thing in the world is thought, for thought can move swifter than the speed of light. The sweetest thing in the world is sleep, for when you are tired nothing is so sweet. And the richest thing is the earth itself, for all riches spring from the earth."

"Excellent," cried the judge, impressed. "The cow is yours. But tell me, poor farmer, though you repeat them well, from whose lips did those answers originally spring?"

Clever Manka

Surprised that the judge had guessed his secret, the poor farmer admitted that his daughter, Manka, had indeed answered the riddle.

"I'd like to see this daughter of yours," said the judge. "Tell her to come to me. But tell her this: she must not travel by day nor by night, neither on a horse nor on foot, be neither clothed nor unclothed."

When the farmer delivered the message to Manka, she didn't look puzzled, but only smiled. Early the next day, at the crack of dawn, when night had left the sky but day had not yet arrived, she set out for the judge's house, draped only in a fishing net to cover her modesty and perched on the back of an old goat. As she reached his door she called out,

"Here I am, though I have not traveled by day nor by night, neither on a horse nor on foot, and am neither clothed nor unclothed." The judge looked from his window, saw that she was quite right and chuckled that she could solve his riddles so easily. Then he asked her to be his wife.

"But mind, my dear Manka, never use your cleverness to interfere with my work," he cautioned, "or I will return you to your father's house."

Clever Manka

So Manka and the judge were married, and Manka didn't interfere, until one day there came a particularly foolish case before the judge. The dispute involved the owner of a mare that had given birth to a foal in the marketplace, and the owner of a cart under which both the mare and the foal had taken refuge. The owner of the mare declared that of course the foal belonged to him, but the owner of the cart argued that the foal had been found under his cart, and therefore the foal belonged to the cart!

The judge, who was not paying attention, decided that the cart owner was in the right.

When Manka heard the story, she quickly went to the owner of the mare and whispered a plan in his ears, but begged him to keep her involvement a secret.

That afternoon he put Manka's plan into action. He strung a fishing net across the dusty road outside of the judge's courtroom and then stood hauling in and then throwing out the net until he had the judge's attention.

"What on earth are you doing?" asked the Judge.

"I'm fishing, of course," replied the man. "Dear sir, you have as much chance of catching a fish in a dusty road as you have of finding birds at the bottom of the sea," said the judge. "Really?" replied the man. "I thought my chances were as high as a cart giving birth to a foal."

The judge, recognizing the owner of the mare, realized his error, and declared him the rightful owner of the foal. But the judge was not deceived. He detected his wife's hand in this, and so he went to her immediately.

"Manka, I warned you that if you used your cleverness to interfere with my work I would send you back to your father. And, though I love you dearly, I must keep to my word. But you shall not accuse me of stinginess, so you may take with you the one thing you value most in the house."

"Very well," said Manka, I will return to my father's house with only the one thing I value. But first I beg you, let us eat supper together one last time.

The judge agreed, and so Manka prepared a supper of the finest dishes she knew, accompanied by the very finest wine, the one her husband liked best. The supper was delicious, and the more the judge ate, the more he drank, and the more he drank, the sleepier he felt until finally he fell into a deep sleep.

Before he could stir, Manka bade the servants carry her husband to a waiting wagon, and then drove them to the poor cottage of her father, where the judge found himself the next morning.

"Why am I here" the judge gasped in surprise. "Why am I not in my own bed?"

"Why, Husband," replied Manka, "you told me I could take with me the one thing I valued most in the house, and so here you are."

The judge could only smile. It wasn't the first time Manka had got the better of him, and it wouldn't be the last. From that day on he always asked Manka's advice whenever a new case came before him, and he never tried to send her away again.

The Robot Nan

Every Wednesday, Olive and Erica's Nan picked them up from school. This particular Wednesday, Erica's teacher Mrs. Williams brought Erica out, her face spotted with orange and blue paint.

"I'm sorry Erica is late," said Mrs. Williams. "She wanted to finish what she was doing."

"And what was that?" laughed Nan. "Having a paint fight?"

"Certainly not," sighed Erica. "I was inventing a flying machine. But I just can't get it to work."

The Robot Nan

Olive was waiting on a bench in the playground, kicking her legs angrily. "You're always late," she grouched.

"Inventing a flying machine takes time," grinned Erica.

"Why bother with a flying machine?" said Olive, watching her Nan walk slowly towards them. "Why not invent something more useful?"

Nan lived in a ground-floor apartment across town. Olive slipped her arm through her Nan's to walk the short distance from the bus stop. Erica ran ahead, hiding behind lamp posts. "Chase me, Nan!" she puffed.

"Ssh!" whispered Olive, elbowing her younger sister. "Nan can't run."

Nan peered into her big, silver handbag, looking for keys. "I want to run," she said, "and climb trees. But when I was around your age, Erica, my bones and joints started misbehaving. Sometimes it's difficult to move around."

"If your bones aren't behaving," frowned Erica, "you should put them on 'time out.'" Nan chuckled. "They were on 'time out' for a long time," she said. "They didn't trouble me for years. But now they've started being misbehaving again . . . Olive, could you please unlock the door for me?"

The Robot Nan

Inside, the girls flung off their shoes and ran straight to the kitchen. Olive filled the kettle and Erica stood on a stool to retrieve a tin marked "Cake"
"Brownies," said Erica, looking inside. "Yummy."

The doors between the living room and garden were open. Herby scents wafted in. Nan was sitting outside, waiting. "Tea, cake… what's missing?" she smiled.

Erica scurried out. She returned clutching an old-fashioned spinning top. Faded pictures and scratches suggested the toy had been well-used.
"Whose turn is it?" teased Nan.
"Mine!" Olive grabbed the top from Erica's hands and pumped the handle. Painted figures danced in a circle, quicker and quicker until the patterns merged into a pale silver stream.
"It's humming!" Erica yelled excitedly. "Come on, Nan."
"Ready?" The girls nodded eagerly. Nan started. "I have a spinning top that . . ."
". . . takes me back in time," the girls joined in.

Every Wednesday, they spun the top and Nan told a story about her Caribbean childhood. It was funny imagining their grandmother as a naughty girl chasing chickens or catching tadpoles in the bamboo-fringed streams. But this Wednesday Nan surprised them.
"I have a spinning top that . . . takes me forward in time," she said.
Erica and Olive looked at each other.
"A long, long way forward, when I'm a robot nan with hands of steel and arms that ping in and out. I can walk forever and jump so high that my eyebrows reach the clouds."
"Robots don't have eyebrows," said Olive uncertainly. "This one does," said Nan. "And she has two brave assistants called Erica and Olive."

The girls' father came for them at seven o'clock. "What was the story today?" he asked, as they drove across town. "Did she chase the enormous black toad from the porch? Or was it when the anaconda fell on Granddad's head?"
"She was a robot," said Olive. "With super-strong arms and legs."

"But that's not true," said Erica. 'cause her fingers hurt so much today that Olive had to unlock the front door."

For the next two days, Erica's room was full of crumpled drawings and she refused to explain what they were. Olive grew impatient. "Forget about your silly flying machine!" But Erica just smiled mysteriously.

Olive finally banged on her door, she was desperate to know what Erica was up to. "Erica, please let me in," she begged. The bedroom door opened a sliver. A long piece of paper fluttered from Erica's fingers. "If you want to help with my invention, this is what I need!"

Olive looked at the list and sighed. It took all morning and much pleading with her parents to find everything, "why do you need Dad's luggage wheels?" she complained. "And a mop or old bicycle clips? I had to open my birthday science kit to get you a magnet, so I definitely want that back. Sewing stuff, plastic gloves. Dad's gone out for plaster of Paris and says there are no old sheets, but you can have this curtain. This is going to be the weirdest flying machine ever!" "It's not a flying machine," beamed Erica. "Look!"

Olive looked. "Wow!" she said, and followed Erica into the bedroom.

The Robot Nan

Nan came for lunch on Sunday. The girls busied themselves with the final details of Erica's invention.

"Ready?" their mother was outside the bedroom. The door opened. Erica wore one of Dad's old white shirts, like a scientist's coat. Olive held a clipboard and pen. Their mother stared into the room. "I'd better help you carry it downstairs!" she laughed.

Nan was sitting with Dad at the garden table.
"So the world's two best inventors have been at work all weekend!" she said. Erica ran up and hugged her. "Yes, and we've made something especially for you!"

Their mother placed the covered object carefully on the ground. Erica whipped off the blanket. Olive's old school backpack was tied to luggage wheels and decorated with pom-poms.
"A wheely bag!" said Nan. "Wonderful!"

"That's just the carrying case," Olive explained. "Look inside!"

Nan reached in and pulled out the mop pole. A bicycle clip was tied to the end instead of the mop head. Nan pushed the button on the handle that made the pole longer. She chuckled. Then she laughed and wiped her eyes. Erica and Olive looked at each other uncertainly.

"Do you know what it is, Nan?" asked Olive

"Of course." Nan waved the pole in the air. "It's my robot arm!"

"Yes," said Erica excitedly. "The bicycle clip can hold a can while you open it." Olive delved into the backpack-on-wheels.

"We made the arm so you can add on different things." She laid a bright red magnet on the table. "This is to find pins or paperclips."

Nan picked up a plaster of Paris hand that had a pointing forefinger.

The girls had glued ribbons on it so that it could be tied around the pole.

"You can poke people if they're far away," Erica explained. "And make holes in your garden for worms. I made it by pouring plaster of Paris into a rubber glove."

Nan tied the hand to the pole. "Now I really am a Robot Nan!" she said.

She pushed the button on the stick so the end flew out and the plaster finger poked Dad's shoulder.

"Robot pointy-thing alert!" he laughed.

Nan put an arm around the girls' shoulders and gathered them in for a hug.

"Ready for another Robot Nan story?" she asked.

"Well . . ." said Erica.

"We would rather hear about when you were little," finished Olive.

Nan lay the robot arm on the table and slowly straightened her fingers.

"Have I told you about the spider as big as a bird?" she asked.

"No," squealed the girls. "Tell us!"

The Six Swans

Once upon a time, there lived a King who had one daughter and six sons. The King loved his children very much, for his wife had died many years earlier and they were the only relations he had left in the world.

One day, the King went hunting. He rode deeper and deeper into the woods following a stag, until all at once he realized he was lost. Each way he turned the paths looked the same. He grew more and more worried until suddenly he spotted an old woman sitting on a tree trunk.

"Excuse me," said the King politely. "Could you show me the way out of the woods so I can find my way home?"

The woman saw his royal robes and realized at once that he was a King. "I will show you on one condition," she answered slyly. "You must marry my beautiful daughter and take her to be Queen of your land."

"And what if I do not care to take the hand of your daughter?" asked the King. "Then I will leave you alone for the wild animals to hunt!" she replied.

The King was worried about his children, so he was forced to agree.

The next day the King kept his word and married the woman's daughter. But he saw that she would not be a kind stepmother to his children, so he asked his servants to hide his family in a castle, deep in the oak forest.

Every morning, before the sun rose, the King left his wife sleeping and went to visit his children. Then he crept back to his bed before his wife noticed. One day, however, his wife woke early and noticed that he was gone. The same thing happened the next morning. She became suspicious and decided to follow him.

121

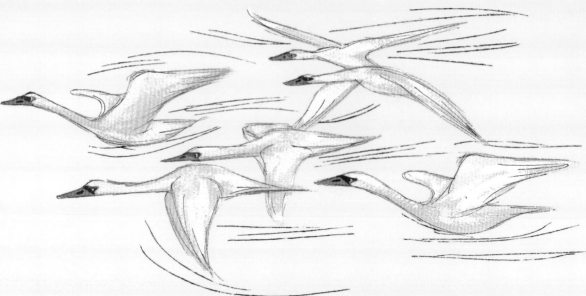

On seeing that he had seven children hiding in a castle, the Queen became very angry. She took a ball of magic string she had been given by her mother and, using a spell she had learned from her, turned the string into magic shirts made of pure white silk.

The next time the King went out hunting, the evil Queen hurried to the castle in the oak forest. Thinking it was their father arriving, the six boys rushed outside to greet him. Immediately, the Queen threw the magic shirts over them. At once, the six boys were turned into six white swans, and all flew away.

When the King went to visit his children the next morning, only his daughter remained. He was heartbroken when she told him what had happened. "You must stay here until I can find a new, safe place to hide you," he told her.

That night, as the winds howled, the daughter was sure she heard her brothers calling in the forest, so she left the castle to look for them. All night she searched and searched, until she could go no further.

At last she spotted a hut.
"Maybe I can shelter here," she thought, opening the door. Inside she saw six beds. She longed to lie down, but she was worried that the owners might return, so she hid herself under one and closed her eyes to sleep.

The Six Swans

The girl was woken by the sound of beating wings. Opening her eyes, she was amazed to see six swans land on the beds. As each landed, its feathers fell off, revealing her six handsome young brothers.

"My brothers!" she cried, climbing out from under the bed.

They were overjoyed to see each her, and they all hugged tightly. But the brothers were worried, too.

"You must not stay here," they told her. "This hut isn't safe. We cannot protect you, for we are only human for a few moments each day before we turn back into swans."

"There must be something I can do to help?" said their sister.

"There is," replied her oldest brother, "but it will not be easy. For six years you must not speak or laugh. And in your solitude you must sew six shirts made of the tiniest flower petals."

Before another word could be spoken, the six brothers turned back into swans and flew away. At once, their sister set off in search of the tiniest flowers she could find. Her search took her to another kingdom, where a carpet of the daintiest flowers she had ever seen grew on the forest floor. There she sat down and began to sew.

The next day the King of the land passed by.
"What are you sewing with my prettiest flowers?" he questioned. But the girl could not speak, of course, so she just kept on sewing.

The King was enchanted by this beautiful silent girl who sewed so diligently. He visited her every day, and every day he fell a little more in love with her.

The Six Swans

Before the summer was over, he had persuaded her to marry him, even though she had never spoken a word.

The King's mother did not like this new, silent girl. So she decided upon a plan to get rid of her. After the girl gave birth to the King's first child, the mother stole the baby and spread lies that the girl had given it away. The young Queen's heart was broken, but she could not speak to say what had happened, so she just carried on sewing. The King, who loved his wife, refused to believe the lies.

When the young Queen had another child and it too went missing, the evil mother demanded that her son take action. But the King still loved his wife dearly, and knew in his heart that she would never give away their child. When the third child went missing, however, the King began to doubt his heart. "My wife wants to do nothing more than sew all day long, every day," he thought. "Perhaps my mother is right about her."

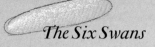

"Surely, if your wife is not guilty then she would tell you so," said the evil mother. Of course, the young Queen could not speak the truth, or any other words, so the King mistrusted his heart and decided she should be punished.

The next day was the day of the Queen's judgment. But it was also the end of the Queen's six years of silence. All through the night she sewed and sewed. By morning she had finished the six shirts, except for the last sleeve of one.

As the Queen stood before the King, her fate to be decided, the air was filled with the noise of beating wings and the trumpeting of swans. At once, the Queen threw the petal shirts over the swans' heads and the spell was finally broken. Before her stood her six brothers, one with a wing of a swan as an arm, for it was that shirt she had not finished in time.

"At last I can speak!" she cried. When the King learned what his mother had done, he sent her away forever. The six brothers took it upon themselves to find their missing nieces and nephews the mother had hidden, and it was to great celebration that they returned home with the missing children. The King was so grateful he invited his wife's brothers to live with them, for their father had passed away in the six years gone.

And so it was that the King, Queen, their children and the six brothers all lived together in happiness for the rest of their lives.

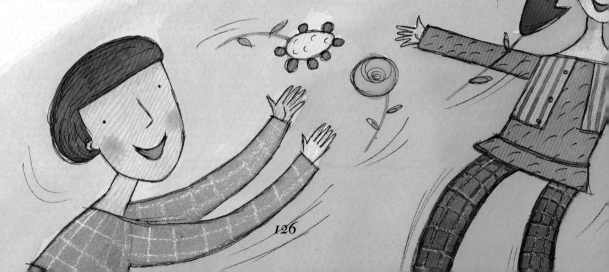

The Bee Wing Ball Gown

Why aren't you drawing Australia?" The teacher's voice made Paula jump. "Even fashion designers must learn geography!"

"Sorry, Mrs. Frazer."

"Let's see!" giggled Paula's best friend, Yasmin. Paula looked around. Mrs. Frazer was at the front of the classroom talking to Josie, the new girl in their class. Paula showed Yasmin her sketch of a wide hat with a feathery plume bending down from the brim.

"You're so good at drawing!" said Yasmin.

Yasmin's mother walked the girls home from school that afternoon. She strode ahead with Yasmin's baby brother, Adam, in his buggy, reading the school newsletter as she walked.

"Have you seen this?" she called, waving the newsletter in the air.

"'This year's play is *Cinderella*,'" she read. "'Come and paint scenery or make up a song. Or take part in our competition to design *Cinderella*'s ball gown. The winning design will become a real dress for the play!'"

Yasmin and Paula hugged each other.

"I've got loads of ideas," said Paula, eyes shining.

"And you can talk about them tomorrow," laughed Yasmin's mother. "Now let's get home."

At school the next morning, Paula fidgeted while the nursery-school children told a story about a troll, accompanied by Mrs. Spender's music class. At last it was time for Mrs. Frazer to read the school news.

"There's a meeting next Wednesday for all *Cinderella* actors and scenery makers. And the ball gown competition is now open for entries. We can only accept entries if you work with a partner."

"Yippee!" whispered Yasmin.

"And the teachers will choose the partners," Mrs. Frazer continued.

There were lots of questions, but Paula didn't hear them. There was no chance that Mrs. Frazer would let her work with Yasmin. Yasmin grabbed Paula's hand. "Maybe we can swap partners," she whispered.

After lunch, Mrs. Frazer announced the pairs. "Yasmin," said Mrs. Frazer. "You're with Maya." Yasmin grinned. Maya loved drawing. She once won a competition for her artwork, so she would be a great help.

"And Paula . . . " Mrs. Frazer consulted her list. "You're with Josie."

Josie? The new girl who never wore dresses and only liked bugs? Paula tried to smile at Josie, but Josie was staring at her desk. Paula turned to Yasmin, but her best friend was chatting excitedly to Maya. Suddenly Paula felt very alone.

That evening, Paula pulled her old fairy tale books from her shelf. She copied some gowns, carefully adding collars and bows, trying out different shades and patterns. She spread the drawings across the kitchen table.

"Very impressive," said Dad. "They could win any competition."

"I can't use them," Paula complained. "My partner's Josie and she's bound not to like anything this girly."

"Well," soothed Dad, sitting down next to her, "no point starting over if you already have something to work with."

"You're right!" Paula added a pink cloak with a furry hem to a ruffled gown. "Josie won't mind if I do most of the work. Then she won't have to do something she hates."

At break the next morning, Paula spotted Josie crouched by a bush. Paula crouched down beside her.

"Ssh," said Josie. "See that ladybug? I don't want to disturb it."

Paula pulled out her drawings.

"Josie, I know you're not really into fashion design. These are for the competition. You pick one and I can enter it for both of us." The ladybug clambered onto a leaf and flew away. Josie looked through the pictures and handed them back. Silence.

"Do you like them?" asked Paula nervously. Josie shook her head.

"Why?" Paula demanded.

"They're just . . . well . . . boring," said Josie quietly.

Paula's eyes prickled. She stuffed the pictures back in her bag, not caring if they wrinkled or tore. "Well, you're boring too! All you're interested in is bugs!"

The Bee Wing Ball Gown

Just after supper, Paula's doorbell rang and she heard the mumble of voices. "Paula?" called her mother.

The woman at the door was tall, with curly hair and a friendly smile. "I'm Josie's mother," she said. "I heard you two had an argument. Would you like to come over for an hour or so?"

Paula hesitated. "You could still win that competition," Paula's mother reminded her.

Josie lived on the sixth floor of a tall building on a busy street. The door opened and Paula stepped into a room that smelled of hot sugar. "We're trying out a new popcorn machine," said Josie. "We can have some later."

Josie pushed open a door. "This is my bedroom."

Paula walked in and immediately jumped out again. A massive spider hung on the wall opposite.

"It's only a poster," laughed Josie. "And most spiders are harmless."

"Don't they bite?"

"Not all," said Josie. "But they do have forty-eight knees."

Paula stared at the picture.

"And worms have five hearts," Josie told her. "But no noses at all."

When Josie's mum brought in the popcorn, the girls were poring over a drawing book.

"Do you copy these from pictures?" Paula was asking.

"Sometimes I watch the insects in the park," said Josie. "And my cousin's got a wormery. You can see the worms moving inside."

Paula stroked a drawing of a bee's wing.

"It's like lace,'" she said. "I can't believe you can draw like this."

"Well I only copy the animals I'm interested in, I guess they're not bad pictures," replied Josie shyly.

133

The final day of the competition arrived. Mrs. Frazer cleared a board to show off the entries. Paula and Josie examined the display. There were about twenty ball gowns. Many had long puffy skirts. Some were decorated with cloaks, others with jewel-encrusted belts. Yasmin's and Maya's was a sweeping gown of gold cloth with scarlet shoes and a sparkly headband.

Paula and Josie's design was nothing like the others. It had red shoes with black spots, leggings as green as a cricket and a shiny, beetle-black top. A floor-length lacy wing fell from each shoulder. The outfit was completed by a pink hat.

"Cinderella's got a worm on her head!" laughed a little boy.
Mrs. Frazer arrived with a man that the children had never seen before.
"Mr. Lee is helping me judge," she said. "He designs costumes for films and plays."
Excitement rippled through the hall. Paula and Josie held hands tightly. So did Yasmin and Maya. The judges examined every picture, whispered together and wrote some notes. Finally, Mr. Lee stepped forward.

"We have a winner," he said. The girls held their breath.
"We loved them all." He paused. "But the winner is . . . Yasmin and Maya."

Yasmin and Maya grinned as everybody clapped. Josie turned to Paula.
"I bet you wish Yasmin was your partner," she said.
"No!" Paula was surprised. "I'm really glad we've become friends."

"Josie? Paula?" Mrs. Frazer beckoned. Mr. Lee was holding their picture.
"This is very different," he said. "Not quite right for Cinderella. But it's perfect for the Carnival Queen Bee leading our procession this year. Can we use it?"
"Yes, please," gasped the girls.
"And you two can ride on the Carnival float," said Mrs. Frazer.

Josie and Paula looked at each other.
"Thank you," said Josie. Paula grinned and clasped Josie's hand. They might not have won the school competition but they were to be in the carnival parade! It couldn't be a better prize!

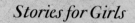

The Fisherman & His Wife

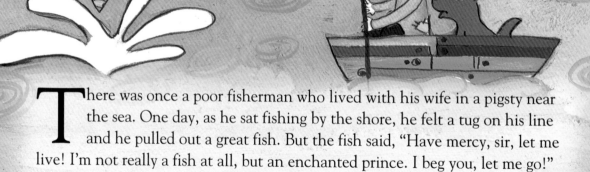

There was once a poor fisherman who lived with his wife in a pigsty near the sea. One day, as he sat fishing by the shore, he felt a tug on his line and he pulled out a great fish. But the fish said, "Have mercy, sir, let me live! I'm not really a fish at all, but an enchanted prince. I beg you, let me go!" The fisherman gasped in surprise, but he did as the fish asked.

When the fisherman returned home he told his wife how he had caught a fish, and how the fish had told him he was really an enchanted prince so he had let it go. "And you asked for no reward in return for his life?" asked the wife. "Go back and tell the fish we want to live in a snug little cottage."

The fisherman didn't like to ask for a reward, but he was afraid of his wife, so he went to the seashore, where the water was calm and blue, and said:

> "O great fish in the sea!
> I beg you, won't you listen to me?
> My wife Isabill
> Must have her own will,
> And has sent me to claim a reward from thee!"

The great fish came swimming to the surface and said, "Well, fisherman, what does your wife desire?"

"Oh!" said the fisherman. "My wife doesn't want to live in a pigsty she wishes for snug little cottage instead."

"Go home, then," said the fish. "She is in the cottage already!"

So the fisherman went home, and in place of the pigsty was a snug little cottage, with his wife standing at the door.

"Is this not better than the pigsty?" she asked, sweeping her arms around the cozy room. And the fisherman had to agree that indeed it was better.

"Now, we shall be happy!" he said.

And so they lived happily for a few weeks, and then one day the wife said, "Husband, there is not enough room in this cottage. I should like to have a large stone castle to live in. Go back to the fish and tell him we'd like a castle to live in instead."

The fisherman didn't like to ask for another reward, but once more he was afraid of his wife, so he went to the seashore, where the sea looked sickly yellow and green. And so he stood at the water's edge and said:

> "O great fish in the sea!
> I beg you, won't you listen to me?
> My wife Isabill
> Must have her own will,
> And has sent me to claim a reward from thee!"

"Well, what does she want now?" asked the fish.

"Oh!" said the fisherman. "My wife wants a large stone castle now."

"Go home, then," said the fish. "She is in the castle already!"

138

The Fisherman & His Wife

So the fisherman went home, and in place of the snug cottage was a large stone castle. Inside the castle the rooms were all furnished with silver chairs and silk carpets. His wife said, "Is this not fine?"
The fisherman had to agree that it was, and said, "Now we shall be happy!"

The next morning the fisherman was woken early by his wife, who said, "Husband, look outside the window. I should like to be King of all that land. Go back to the fish and tell him I'd like to be King."

The fisherman didn't like to ask for yet another reward, but even now he was still afraid of his wife. So he went to the seashore, where the sea was dark and muddy, and the surface was broken by large waves. He stood a little way back from the water's edge and called:

"O great fish in the sea!
I beg you, won't you listen to me?
My wife Isabill
Must have her own will,
And has sent me to claim a reward from thee!"

"Well, what does she want now?" asked the fish.

"Oh!' said the fisherman. "My wife wishes to be King of the land as well."

"Go home, then," said the fish. "She is King already!"

So the fisherman went home, and as he approached the castle he saw that it was guarded by a troop of soldiers, and inside he saw his wife sitting on a golden throne with a crown of rubies upon her head. And his wife said, "I am King. Is it not great to be King?"

And the fisherman had to agree that indeed it was great to be King, and said, "Now we shall be happy!"

But the wife had not been King for more than an hour before she said to the fisherman: "Husband, it is not enough to be King, so I wish to be Emperor as well. Go back to the fish and tell him I'd like to be Emperor.

The fisherman really didn't want to ask for yet another reward, but now his wife was King, so he couldn't refuse. So he went to the seashore, where the sea was black and full of violent waves. He stood quite a way back from the water's edge and cried:

"O great fish in the sea!
I beg you, won't you listen to me?
My wife Isabill
Must have her own will,
And has sent me to claim a reward from thee!"

"Well, what does she want now?" asked the fish.

"Oh!" said the fisherman. "My wife doesn't wish only to be King, she wishes to be Emperor as well."

"Go home, then," said the fish. "She is Emperor already!"

So the fisherman went home once again, and as he walked up the red carpet in the great hall he saw his wife sitting on a huge throne made of diamonds and pearls, with a cloak of mink around her shoulders. And the wife said, "I am Emperor. Is it not tremendous to be Emperor?"

And the fisherman had to agree that indeed it was tremendous to be Emperor, and said, "Now, we shall be happy!"

But that night the fisherman's wife could not sleep. "For all my power as Emperor," she thought, "I do not have the power to make the sun rise in the sky." This vexed her a great deal, and so she woke her husband to speak with him.

She said, "Husband, go to the fish once more and tell him I must be lord of the sun and the moon."

The fisherman was horrified by his wife's demands, but now his wife was Emperor and must be obeyed. So he went to the seashore, where he saw that the the the waves were as tall as mountains and threatened to sweep him into the sea. And so he stood far from the water's edge, and shouted:

"O great fish in the sea!
I beg you, won't you listen to me?
My wife Isabill
Must have her own will,
And has sent me to claim a reward from thee!"

"Well, what does she want now?" asked the fish.

"Oh!" said the fisherman. "My wife wishes to be lord of the sun and the moon."

"Go home, then," said the fish, who had finally had enough. "You'll find that it is a pigsty again!"

And there they live to this very day.

The Butterfly Garden

L ottie, Sam and Michelle were the best of friends. One day, just before school ended for the summer, they were wandering home along the lane that led to their road, when all at once they stopped. Dancing in front of them was the most beautiful butterfly they had ever seen.

"It's so pretty!" whispered Sam. "I wish I was a butterfly."

Another butterfly appeared, then another, and another. There were butterflies everywhere. The three girls watched, enchanted, as the gentle creatures swirled around them then fluttered back up the lane.

"Let's follow them!" cried Lottie, grabbing her friends' hands.

The girls followed the fluttering trail through the park and into the town, until they came to a door in a wall behind the bus stop. The door was slightly ajar.

"Do you think we should follow them?" whispered Michelle.

"Absolutely!" cried Lottie. She grabbed hold of her friends once again and pulled them through before they could protest.

The girls stepped out into a sun-drenched public garden.

"Oh!" gasped Sam. "It's beautiful!"

The velvety lawn was divided by archways dripping with flowers. Right in the middle was a pond with a fountain. Everywhere the girls looked, there were butterflies and other creatures. Birds sang and dragonflies hummed as the girls wandered along the walkways, breathing in the scent of a thousand flowers.

The Butterfly Garden

It was only when they reached the fountain that Lottie found her voice. "I don't think I've ever been anywhere as beautiful as this. I can't believe it was just sitting here in the middle of town all this time."

The girls sat in the garden and looked around for a long time, until their tummies began to rumble and they remembered it was nearly time for supper. Only then did they reluctantly go home.

Lottie, Sam and Michelle visited the garden almost every day that summer. They had picnics, played games, and chatted while watching the butterflies dance around. It was their secret.

One Sunday, towards the end of the summer, Sam was having lunch with her family when something in the conversation made her sit up and pay attention. Sam's dad was talking about a new shopping mall that was going to be built in the middle of town. As she listened, it slowly dawned on Sam where they were planning to build it. They were going to build it right on top of the garden. The news upset Sam so much, she could barely finish her lunch. Afterwards she ran upstairs to her room and burst into tears. Their beautiful secret garden was going to be destroyed. It was more than she could bear.

The Butterfly Garden

Later that day Sam met her friends at the garden as usual, and told them the terrible news.

"We've got to do something!" cried Lottie. "This must be why the butterflies led us here, so that we could save their garden!"

"But what can we do?" asked Michelle. "Who will listen to us?"

Lottie was adamant. "We have to try. We can't let it be destroyed."

All afternoon, the girls discussed ways to save the garden. They felt sure that if others knew how wonderful it was, then maybe they could convince the town council to save it.

"I know," said Lottie. "Why don't we organize a party at the garden?"

"Great idea!" the others agreed. "Then everyone can see how special it is."

The girls spent the rest of the week making invitations, which they mailed to everyone they could think of: friends, parents, teachers – even the mayor.

When the day of the party arrived, the girls spent the whole morning preparing food and drinks for their guests. They borrowed chairs and tables and arranged them around the garden.

Finally they hung banners from the trees that said "Save the Butterfly Garden!"

As the guests arrived, the three friends showed them around, and told them about the shopping mall. "We must save the garden!" they explained. "It doesn't just belong to the town. It belongs to all the creatures that live here too."

Everybody who saw the garden agreed that it had to be saved, and they all signed a petition. Soon the girls had over one hundred signatures. At the end of the afternoon, the girls approached the mayor, who was sitting admiring the fountain.

"Excuse me," said Lottie nervously. "We'd like to present you with our petition to save this garden."

"Thank you," said the mayor kindly, "but I'm afraid that the plans have already been approved. I'm sorry, but the decision is out of my hands at this stage. So, girls, unless you can come up with a miracle, this wonderful garden will be knocked down." And with a sad smile the mayor left.

The girls were devastated. They sat in a corner, unable to believe that they had failed, even with all the signatures and hard work they had put in.

"Never mind," consoled Sam's father. "Maybe there's something else you can do to save the garden. But right now we need to tidy up this mess."

The three girls started to clear up all the leftovers.

The Butterfly Garden

"It's not fair," sighed Michelle, gazing at a blue butterfly, sitting on the rim of a cup she was holding. "Why are buildings more important than a beautiful butterfly like this?"

Lottie turned to look. A strange expression came over her face.

"Don't move, Michelle," she whispered. "Sam! Quick! Bring me my camera. I think that butterfly is a Cornhill Beauty. It's a very rare species. I saw one in my wildlife book the other day."

Sam and Michelle held their breath as Lottie held up the camera and fiddled with the lens. SNAP! She just managed to take a picture before the butterfly fluttered away.

"I think we might just have found our miracle," cried Lottie, grinning from ear to ear. "We can e-mail this picture to the Science Museum. Cornhill Beauties are a protected species!"

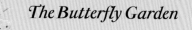

The girls waited anxiously all the following day for a reply to their email. "Maybe they didn't get it!" suggested Sam, after they had checked their in-box for the hundredth time that afternoon. "Let's send it again."
Suddenly, the computer went *ding*.

"We've got mail!" cried Lottie, clicking on her in-box. The three girls eagerly crowded around the computer screen.
"It's from the Science Museum," read Sam. "It *is* a Cornhill Beauty. The head zoologist wants to come and see the garden for himself. He says that if Cornhill Beauties really live there, it must be a protected habitat. The shopping mall will have to be built somewhere else. He is going to speak to the planning department at the town hall right away."

And that's exactly what happened. It wasn't long before the local newspapers were full of the story about Lottie, Michelle and Sam, and how they had saved the garden from demolition. The girls even received a letter from the mayor, thanking them for all their hard work.

The Butterfly Garden

"Our garden is going to be renamed," said Lottie, as she read the letter out loud. It's going to be called The Butterfly Garden."

Now the whole town enjoys The Butterfly Garden. But nobody loves it more than Lottie, Sam and Michelle. To this day, they hold a party there every summer, to celebrate its rescue, and to remind everyone how just how special it is.

The Little Mermaid

Far beneath the clear blue waves, the Little Mermaid lived in her father's kingdom with her five sisters and her grandmother. She was the youngest of her sisters, and the loveliest of them all. Her beautiful voice carried far across the water as she sang happily to herself.

More than anything else, the Little Mermaid loved to listen to her grandmother as she told tales of the world above the sea. She was mesmerized by her grandmother's descriptions of human beings and their ships, of the birds that flew high in the sky and the busy towns by the seashore. But it would be some years before the Little Mermaid could discover these things for herself; for a mermaid had to be fifteen before she was allowed to rise to the surface to see these extraordinary sights.

One by one, as they reached their fifteenth birthday, the Little Mermaid's sisters made the journey to the world above the ocean and came back with wonderful stories of what they had seen. The Little Mermaid longed to see these things for herself and waited impatiently for her fifteenth birthday.

On the day she turned fifteen, she could barely contain her excitement as she held on to her sisters hands and they started to swim towards the surface.

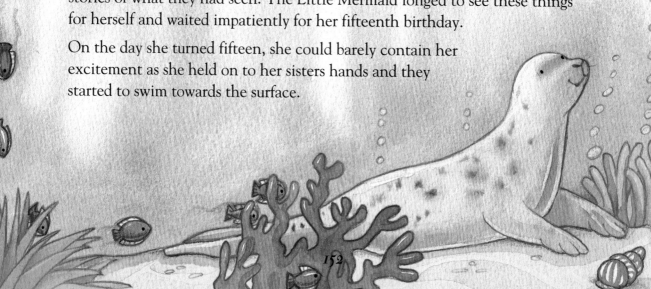

153

As her head popped above the waves for the first time, the Little Mermaid gasped – for the sun's rays glittered on the water and the clouds glowed pink and gold. It was the most beautiful thing the Little Mermaid had ever seen.

Suddenly, the peaceful scene was shattered by a loud explosion. There before her was a ship, lit up by fireworks in the sky. Laughter drifted across the water. On board the ship a party was under way to celebrate a young Prince's birthday. The Little Mermaid watched as the humans danced on the deck. She gazed at the handsome Prince and imagined herself twirling around in his arms.

As the celebrations went on, the calm seas gave way to waves. They were gentle at first, but the wind grew stronger and soon huge waves were crashing onto the decks of the boat. With a terrifying groan, the deck split in two and the ship began to break up in the swirling waters.

The Little Mermaid

The Little Mermaid watched in horror as the handsome young Prince was thrown into the churning sea. At first he swam against the waves, but soon he grew tired and slipped beneath the surface. Down, down, down he sank. "I must save him," cried the Little Mermaid. With a flick of her tail, she dived beneath the heaving waves and scooped up the young man in her arms.

The Prince was heavy and at times the Little Mermaid feared she would never reach the surface, but finally the waves parted and the Little Mermaid felt the wind on her cheeks once again. She held the Prince tightly in her arms and allowed the waves to carry them towards the shore. Just as the first rays of the sun peeped above the horizon, the Little Mermaid felt sand under her tail.

The little Mermaid stayed with the Prince on the beach for as long as she dared, singing to him softly. But as the sun's rays grew stronger, she knew that she had to return to the water.

The Little Mermaid

The Little Mermaid could not stop thinking about the handsome Prince. Every day she sat on the rocks in the bay to watch him walking in the palace gardens. At first this was enough, but after a while she longed to speak with him.

"But that will never happen," she sighed. "I'll never be human."

"You could be, if you wanted," said a voice next to her. The Little Mermaid turned to find herself face to face with a Sea Fairy. The Little Mermaid hesitated. Sea Fairies were always trouble! But then again, she did seem to know of a way that the Little Mermaid could be human . . .

Ignoring her doubts, the Little Mermaid followed the Sea Fairy.

"I have a potion that will change your tail into legs so you can walk with your Prince," cackled the Sea Fairy. "If you can make him fall in love with you before the sun sets on the second day, you will become human forever. If you fail, you will become a mermaid once more, but must serve me for all eternity!"

The Little Mermaid nodded her agreement as the Sea Fairy passed her a small bottle containing the powerful potion.

The Little Mermaid swam slowly towards the surface with the potion bottle held tightly in her hand. Finally she reached the shore, and sat on the sandy beach below the palace on the cliff. With trembling hands, she uncorked the potion. It smelled terrible!

Shutting her eyes, she put the bottle to her lips and quickly drank the liquid. Her throat burned and her eyes watered, but it was soon forgotten as the Little Mermaid saw her tail change before her very eyes into two pale legs. Very slowly, she stood up and took her first wobbly steps.

Meanwhile, at the palace, the Prince was gazing far out to sea, thinking about the mysterious girl who had rescued him.
"All I can remember is that she had a beautiful singing voice," he told his servant. "If only I could find her. I long to hear her voice again."

Just then, the Prince's servant spotted a bedraggled girl walking up the cliff path. "She must be a survivor from the shipwreck," cried the Prince. "Bring her into the palace and take care of her." He did not recognize the Little Mermaid.

The Little Mermaid was overjoyed to be invited into the palace – especially when she found herself sitting next to the handsome Prince at dinner. But her happiness was short-lived. For at the meal she heard something terrible. A princess from the nearby kingdom was arriving the next day. The Prince's parents wanted him to marry her.

With a heavy heart, the Little Mermaid retired to her bed. It seemed that tomorrow she would have return to the sea to spend her days serving the Sea Fairy.

As dawn broke the next day, a fanfare announced the arrival of the Princess's ship. The Little Mermaid watched from her balcony as the sails grew larger on the horizon. As the ship got nearer, the Prince prepared to sail out to meet his very special guest.
"Come with me," he asked the Little Mermaid. "I would like you to meet her."

The Little Mermaid made her way down the palace steps and climbed aboard the boat. The boat skimmed across the water and soon it was alongside the Princess's ship. Seeing the Princess, the Little Mermaid was filled with dismay.

She was very beautiful. Her dark, silky hair shone in the sunshine and her eyes sparkled as she gazed at the Prince. The Little Mermaid was certain she had lost her Prince forever!

The Little Mermaid

Celebrations lasted for the rest of the day, but the Little Mermaid could not join in. How could she celebrate, when her Prince was to marry another? Soon the sun would dip behind the horizon, and she must return to the sea to become a slave.

Suddenly the Little Mermaid heard a splash. She looked up, it was her sisters! "All is not lost," they told her, when they heard their sister's tale. "We heard the Prince's servant say his master longs to hear the voice of the girl who rescued him. You must sing, sing with all your heart!"

So, as the sun began to set, the Little Mermaid sang the song she had sung to the Prince on the beach. The haunting melody drifted across the sands to where the Prince was standing. At once, he rushed over to the Little Mermaid and embraced her.

"It was you who saved me," he cried, planting a kiss her on her cheek. "I have searched for you everywhere! I will never let you go again!"

Just at that moment, the sun dipped behind the horizon. The spell was broken and the Little Mermaid's wish had come true – she would be human forever and stay with her handsome Prince!